All the Lights That Have Shone

Paul McCormack

Ichabod Dozer Press

ISBN 978-0-9854620-4-8

Table of Contents:

Introduction

This is actually my second attempt at an introduction.

The first was dreadfully depressing: I recounted the pain of losing people I loved in the interim between these stories and the previous collection. It went on and on about how I quit writing because the world didn't seem worth injecting any more of my soul into, etc. etc. Like I said, it was depressing, and worse, rather dull.

While the tone of this collection is less glib than my previous work, I think that the mysteries, wonders and brilliant absurdity in this life still capture my imagination. So let me preface it with this:

This book is a miracle.

Not a "parting of the Red Sea" kind of miracle, more of a "bread landing butter-side-up for once" sort of miracle. The best I explain it is to steal from the life of a friend:

I have a friend who is an artist. Due to forces beyond his control he was chased from his home, abandoned by many of his closest friends and was left (metaphorically and literally) in the wilderness. During this period of exile he dove headlong into his work. All the isolation, fear, loneliness and illness came together inside him and poured onto his canvas.

When he finally was able to return home he gathered his works on the floor to get them ready for shipping and surveyed them. They were a thing of beauty—a testament to strength, vision and tenacity that he didn't even know he had. He described it as a moment where he felt his essence expand—he'd taken the horrible things that had happened and turned them into something beautiful. That process had made him something greater than he had been. Usually just enduring ugliness and pain grows us as human beings, but there are those rare instances where we're able to cultivate it and, through our work, are able to become something exponentially greater than we were.

I would say his work during that period was a "parting of the Red Sea" kind of miracle.

I don't pretend to have overcome anything close to the trials and tribulations he has or even to have produced in these stories anything as visceral and poetic as those paintings. I would say when they're at their best the stories in this collection do offer little snapshots of grace and beauty. Maybe they are a little preoccupied with loss and disappointment, but I think there's enough truth in it that you can still laugh at. I think there is a certain liberation in laughing at failure—especially your own.

As far as the stories themselves, there are sad ones, funny ones (or at least funny-ish, I hope), thoughtful ones and one with a talking dog—you know, for the kids. Hopefully they each can provide amusement on a number of different levels. I'm not sure where all of the inspiration and cautious optimism in them came from, but if I've learned anything, it's that you have to cherish those little stolen moments of grace that you're granted. These stories are the result of a thousand stolen moments—a collection of the kindnesses of friends and strangers alike. I guess I dropped the bread, but it landed butter-side-up for once.

I must acknowledge the following:

Brent & Adina: You opened your home when I needed a place to go, lent your ears when I needed to be heard and have never waivered in your honesty, support and friendship.

John: Part cheerleader, part drill sergeant. I am eternally indebted to you for your encouragement, insight and example—you're a true warrior-poet.

Jason and Jenelle: A life raft when I desperately needed saving.

Lisa: You're a trusted friend whose compassion can only be matched be your integrity.

Vanessa: Not the muse I deserved, but the muse I needed.

AMK: Often I measure my accomplishments by what I've lost rather than what I have. In either measure you've enriched my life in the best possible way. You're truly a beautiful soul.

Kari: One of the best human beings I've ever had the pleasure of meeting. Your enthusiasm, willful optimism and kindness are extraordinary.

Virgil: The best friend, four-legged or otherwise, I could have ever asked for. He will be missed.

Thank you all.

Paul McCormack
19.November.2011

Iodine

for Vanessa

"You see, people think things are a certain way. But if you look at them, even just a little, you see that they're wrong," his voice had that tone again. Grant usually had a very thoughtful, even cadence when he talked, but when he'd get into something that would change. The best description Beth had heard was from her sister: when Grant got worked up his voice sounded like Cathy Corrin's eyes looked when she started talking about eating meat.

Cathy had been Beth's college roommate sophomore year. They got on quite well for the most part, but she was passionate (her word) about veganism. When someone ate meat in her presence, spoke about eating meat, or smelled of something resembling meat there was a 50/50 chance that she would get the "insane-o crazy psycho bitch stare." Beth didn't remember who coined the description, but it stuck and Cathy was either oblivious to the fact she was doing it or flaunted it like it was a badge of honor (depending on the day).

She had incredibly clear, light blue eyes that seemed almost unnaturally large for her face. When the stare kicked in, they'd seem to miraculously grow even larger, her pupils would dilate and the rest of her face would seemingly freeze in a strange zombie-like expression. It was incredibly unnerving, especially if she didn't say anything. If she freaked out and started arguing and declaring how meat was immoral it actually made it a bit better. When she was silent it was like she was waiting for an unguarded moment to pounce and rip out your jugular with her teeth.

Grant's voice had that same uncanny warbling intensity. It wasn't that he was crazy, but when you heard it, it was a pretty fair guess that you weren't about to care nearly as much about the topic as he did.

"No, hear me out on this. It's all through western civilization—how many slaves did Abraham Lincoln free with the Emancipation Proclamation?"

"I don't know," Beth answered. Guessing would have only made it worse, anyway.

"Zero. None. Not a single fucking slave. But what did they tell you in school? Abe Lincoln freed the slaves."

"Well, it did happen as a result of things that occurred while he was in office—" even as the words were spilling out she realized that her input, even if correct, wasn't particularly welcome.

"But he couldn't have known that. He was guessing. He was posturing and hoping to prevent the war that eventually accomplished what he was afraid to do beforehand."

Beth just took a drink and nodded.

"I mean, it's crazy, right? I mean it's even in the Bible." It usually ended up with either religion or vast international conspiracies. Although the fact he'd gotten to the Bible already meant this was likely going to be one of his shorter diatribes.

"Look at the creation story. What's the creation story about?"

There was a pause until Beth realized it wasn't a purely rhetorical question but he was awaiting some sort of response.

"Um, about how the world was made?"

"See, that's what they always say, but let's look at it. The creation of the universe? Sixteen verses, or something like that. It's only the first chapter. The rest of it? It's the Garden of Eden and Noah's Ark and all that stuff. They didn't care about how a tree got to be there. That's just a footnote that said 'there wasn't stuff, now there is.'" Grant was gesturing frantically now, his voice getting higher pitched and almost squeaky.

"No, the question of Genesis isn't 'how did we get here,' it's 'why are we always unhappy?' I mean, think about it:

when you look at origin myths you think of these big grandiose stories of gods creating things and fighting and bringing humanity into the world to do whatever. They try to explain why there's lightening or where fire came from or whatever. In Genesis they just mention that in passing and then launch right into the story of getting kicked out of the Garden of Eden. They wanted to explain why things were horrible and the only explanation they could fathom was that we did something to deserve it. And then the rest of the book launches into murder and incest and God trying to wipe the slate clean and start again. I mean how the fuck is that a way to start a religion?"

He took a swig of beer. "They don't point that out. They don't like to see that. They like to think it's a story about how everything was made and a snake. That's what they tell kids because how do you explain to a four year-old that the story is about how people have been unhappy since the dawn of time and if there is a God it's that way by design.

"So what do they do? Demonize apples. Fucking apples! It wasn't even an apple in the Garden of Eden. It was a fucking pomegranate or some damn thing."

There was silence for a few moments. It was like an earthquake—you should stay sheltered until you were sure it was over but even then you had to be wary of aftershocks. Grant likewise would usually have a few minor rants in the ensuing hours.

Beth had learned that even if he sounded upset it was never directed at her specifically. When they had first started seeing each other his occasional random outbursts were fun. Sometimes she'd even egg him on to see how grandiose and over the top she could get him to go. He picked up on it most of the time and it became a game.

It was different now. A lot of things were different now.

That night as he finished, body tense and breath ragged, she held the back of his head to her chest and closed her eyes. Even now he seemed far away. She hooked her leg around him keeping him inside her, keeping him near. She used to love this part: the eye contact, the feel of him seeping out of her, the breathy smiles and the little squeezes and motions they'd both use to prolong the other's pleasure. But he wouldn't look her in the eyes anymore. She tried to wrap her limbs around him to keep him with her, but he just rolled off her onto his back. She followed him over, lying on her side watching him.

"I have to get up early," he said. That was his way of saying he didn't want to talk. He grabbed a corner of the sheet and turned onto his side, his back to her. She reached out to touch him, but thought better of it at the last moment. She let her hand fall to bed where he had been lying. The sheet still felt warm. Her hand was close enough to him to feel the static-y warmth from his body, but it didn't comfort her. She was inches away from him but it might as well have been an ocean.

She didn't mind the ups and downs. Their relationship had its share but they'd made it through. When he got wrapped up in vast conspiracies and the injustices of the world she'd been able to bring him back to Earth. When she had been insecure Grant's quiet reassurance had turned the mountains back into molehills. He'd been good for her and they'd been good for each other. But now she didn't know what to do.

The worst part was waking up in the middle of the night to him crying. He cried in his sleep most nights. The first few times it happened she woke him but it didn't seem to help. Instead he'd lie restlessly next to her unable to get back to sleep. He wouldn't talk about it, but she knew who it was about. She would have known even if she hadn't heard him quietly sobbing her name in his sleep: Lorna.

Lorna was his older sister, but their relationship was different than any brother and sister she had known. Grant was five when they adopted Lorna. Lorna had been nine at the time. Grant was unsure of what to make of her at first. His mother said that he barely spoke to Lorna the first month, but Lorna adored Grant immediately. When Grant didn't respond to her she didn't force anything.

"It was the sweetest thing," his mother Shirley told her once, "She'd do these little things she knew he'd notice. Like if we were all watching the television she'd ask to watch his favorite program even though I don't think she really cared for it. She'd clean up after him and help him with his chores if he wanted to go out and play. Stuff like that.

"I didn't know if Grant would ever like her. I felt bad for her some days because she'd be doing all these things for him and he wouldn't say boo. I told her she didn't have to do that and that Grant should do his own chores. She told me, and I remember this, 'It's ok. He doesn't know how to have a sister yet. I'm just helping him.' I mean, it was either the sweetest thing I'd ever heard or the silliest. But she loved that boy.

"She came down with chicken pox that fall and I remember she got so sick. We thought we were going to have to take her to the hospital she was so bad. She was real bad the night right before it finally broke. I came up to check on her and Grant was standing just inside her door.

"He was supposed to be asleep and I was going to tell him to get to bed but when I got to him he was just crying and crying. Not so loud so anyone could hear, but I'd never seen him cry like that before. I gave him a hug and told him Lorna would be ok and he should go back to bed. He didn't say a word and I carried him back to his bed the whole time he was just crying in those little gasps like you do when you just can't stop. It just broke my heart.

"Well, the next morning Lorna was doing better and Grant was a completely different little boy. They were inseparable after that. It was the darndest thing."

Beth had answered the phone when Grant's father Clell called with the news. Lorna had been on a cruise—Grant used to make fun of her for taking trips that only old people would take. The cruise had been just the latest example, but she'd taken bus tours to Branson, train trips to Vancouver, just about any cliché you could think of. Grant always ribbed her about playing shuffleboard and buffet lines. She laughed at his little jabs good-naturedly. She never explained what appeal she saw in them but she always became giddy—like a child the night before their birthday giddy—when she was about to leave.

There wasn't anything special about the cruise; it was just a seven-day trip through the Caribbean. She said she'd buy Beth one of those necklaces made out of little seashells when they'd talked on the phone the night before her departure. And then she was gone.

That was the worst part for everyone. She was just gone. The cruise line said they didn't suspect any foul play, and the FBI hadn't found anything either. The third night she had been out on the deck and she either fell or jumped. There wasn't a note and Shirley insisted something had happened, but there was no way to tell. There was no body. There were no witnesses. There was a duffle bag and a suitcase that the FBI returned a few weeks later and that was it. The luggage was the only evidence she wasn't coming home.

They'd waited by their phones secretly hoping there had been a mistake or that a passing fishing boat would find her alive and well. Beth was pretty sure Shirley still did even now, but the others had, one by one, slowly come to the inevitable conclusion.

They had all been at Clell and Shirley's house one evening a week after the luggage had been returned. Beth was sitting in the living room, Clell sat across from her next to the picture window. Grant, Shirley and Grant's grandmother Agnes were in the kitchen talking in hushed tones. Clell was looking out the window watching some squirrels chasing each other away from the bird feeders.

"We can't keep doing this. She wouldn't want it to be like this," he said quietly like he was talking to himself.

At dinner he announced that he was going to arrange a memorial service. No one said anything. Shirley began sobbing quietly but other than that everyone sat silently, looking at their empty plates wondering how much they'd have to eat to be polite even though they weren't hungry.

The service had been on a Thursday. Beth had hoped it would rain or at least be overcast—something to reflect what was happening, but it had been a perfectly average late spring morning. It was all too eerily normal for Beth. There should've been something to acknowledge that everything had changed, she thought.

Before the service started Beth and Grant had been mulling around in the lobby of the church, shaking hands with near strangers who gave their condolences.

"She's not here. She should be here," Grant had whispered to her. "It's like a birthday party for someone who isn't going to be there. There's just no point to it. How are we supposed to act like we don't think she's out there somewhere? We should be trying to find her, to bring her home so we can do this right."

The change in him was pronounced. When they were still holding out hope he'd call from work to see if there'd been any news. He came straight home and sat by the phone often checking it to make sure the phone hadn't died or that the line was open. Then one day it just stopped. For the better part of a month Beth barely had a chance to remember what the phone's ringer sounded like because Grant answered it at the slightest chirp. Now he didn't even stir if it rang. Most of the time either Beth would have to answer it or it would go to voicemail.

In 10th grade Beth's science teacher showed them a video in class. A man in a lab coat put a piece of crystal iodine in a flask and put a stopper on it. Some heat was applied to the flask and a purple cloud billowed up inside. The voiceover explained how some substances could go directly from solid to gaseous form through sublimation and the purple cloud was actually iodine in gaseous form.

That's what had happened; Lorna had been sublimated. She'd gone from the tall, lithe black-haired woman with glasses that made her look like a librarian and turned into a cloud hanging over everyone. There was just a "poof" and she disappeared into the atmosphere.

It was happening to Grant, too. He'd sit expressionless watching television. He'd barely speak aside from his random outbursts. He was vanishing into thin air bit by bit too and there was nothing Beth could do about it.

She stared at his back, the sheet pulled over his shoulder like a cape. She couldn't tell if he was sleeping or not. She tried not to disturb him as she fumbled under the covers for her panties. They had been hooked around her right foot but during the final moments they'd slipped free and were now hiding, blending chameleon-like with the sheets. She finally gave up and gently rolled out of bed and got a fresh pair from the drawer.

She stood for a moment unable to convince herself that she wanted to go back to bed. She was tired, but being next to him made her feel even lonelier. She didn't know how she could feel so much for him when he seemed so far away from her. He stirred. At least she knew he was asleep.

She went into the kitchen and made a cup of herbal tea. She'd hoped it would make her tired enough that the twisting knotted feeling in her stomach wouldn't be able to keep her awake. She opened the newspaper from the day before and skimmed the stories she hadn't cared enough to read the first time. None of it helped, but she felt like she was pretending in hopes that at some point it would be true.

She'd re-read the same article on the European Union bailout of Greece three times without having an idea what it said. The words stood as alone, unconnected, trees rather than a forest. Greece. Indicators. Markets. Euro. She tried to wrap her head around them. They didn't seem to mean anything. They were oaks sitting stolid and unmoving. They were pretty in their own way.

"Hey," Grant mumbled from doorway. It startled Beth and she jumped a little. Grant must have noticed because he followed with a quiet, "Sorry."

"Did I wake you?"

"No. I just woke up and you weren't there."

"Couldn't sleep," she answered sheepishly.

He stood looking as if he had something to say.

"Everything ok?" she asked.

"Yeah… Yeah it's fine…" his voice trailed off. He looked lost.

"You want to come back to bed?" he asked finally.

She smiled and nodded.

"Okay. I'll be there in a minute," she said.

The Best of Right Now

for John

Jorge had to wear big thick sunglasses whenever he went out. It didn't seem like a good look for the Today show.

"Jesus, I look like a goddamn drug dealer."

"You don't look like a drug dealer. You look fine."

"You're right, not a drug dealer—I look like one of those actors that wear sunglasses because they think it makes them look less strung out."

"Oh hush," Monica straightened out his jacket. Monica was Jorge's attorney.

"Why do I have to do this?" Jorge grumbled.

"You're a hero. Everyone wants to meet you. You're what's best about America right now. And if you play your cards right maybe you can turn this into a reality show."

"I don't want a reality show."

"Shhh. Stop worrying. Besides, reality TV is where the money is now. Think of this as a job interview."

A guy with a clipboard and earpiece came over to them and said to Monica, "They're almost ready for him. You need anything?"

"Why are you asking her if she needs anything? I'm the one who's about to have a fucking seizure on national television."

Monica chuckled and patted him on the back as she waved the page off, "He's just got some butterflies. We're fine."

As soon as the page walked away her expression changed. It was just like the one Jorge's first grade teacher Miss Applebaum had whenever she caught him eating glue. "Now you need to get it together. We've both got a lot riding on this."

"Why does everyone treat me like goddamn child whenever you're around?"

"Because you're famous. You're supposed to be important. It's a sign of respect that they don't talk to you. Besides, I'm your representation; it's my job to take care of your needs and handle all busy work and talking. It's all a bunch of details that you wouldn't care about anyway. Trust me; enjoy it because they won't be nice to you forever unless we catch a few more breaks. Now stop being so crabby and get out there and show the world why you're a hero."

Jorge wasn't a hero. He knew he wasn't a hero. The late night talk shows knew he wasn't a hero. The snarky wise-ass kids on the internet knew he wasn't a hero. He was pretty sure that meant the rest of the world knew it, too, but he was a novelty. Novelties always seemed to get better titles than they deserved.

"Coming up next, we have an incredible story. A little girl, three year old Teesha Lewis, fell out of a fifth story window but was rescued when she was caught by a good Samaritan who was just passing by. We'll meet both Teesha and the man who saved her life. All that coming up after the break. Be sure to stay with us."

God, the anchor girl had freakishly white teeth Jorge thought to himself.

Of course the story was bullshit. He hadn't caught anyone anymore than Lou Gehrig invented a disease. He had been on his way to work—a job that he subsequently lost in the aftermath—when he heard a shriek. He looked up just in time to see the blur of an Elmo t-shirt and a flurry of limbs hit him in the face. The doctors said it wasn't the initial strike that did the damage but when he was knocked flat and smacked the back of his head on the pavement.

He remembered hearing a lady was scream and the little girl crying and flopping around on his face. She finally managed to roll off of him like a turtle flipping over off its back. Everything else about the story was according to first hand accounts, since the only thing Jorge remembered after that was waking up in a hospital three days later with a splitting headache, a brain shunt and a neck brace.

They said he'd gotten up after "saving" the little girl and asked if anyone knew the way to San Jose. The crowd was more interested in the little girl, but one helpful soul pointed Jorge due south. Details after that were sketchy, but eight hours later he was taken into custody for wandering through traffic claiming he was Gerald Ford.

When he first woke up there was at least a dozen doctors and nurses huddled around his bed, poking and prodding him. They checked and double-checked and proudly told him that they'd determined through their tests, training and the benefit of their own incredible cleverness that he had brain damage. They'd phrased it a little differently, of course.

The seizures had occurred early on. The physical therapist warned him about depression and irritability, difficulty reading or doing math and a bunch of other things that didn't sound very good. The pills were good, though.

One afternoon after his dose of painkillers there was a rap at his doorway. "Excuse me, but what would you like me to tell the reporters?" asked a nurse who looked sort of like a female version of Col. Klink from "Hogan's Heroes".

Jorge smiled. He liked his pills. "Tell them hi for me," he grinned hazily.

Jorge had made it all of ten minutes through the initial press conference before the flashbulbs and lights caused him to fall out of his chair and flop around on the floor like a trout on the deck of a fishing boat. The nightly news showed the part where he answered questions and was seen by thousands of people. On the other hand, the clip of him seizing on the ground got over a million hits on the internet. One version was synced to "The Reflex" which seemed to be particularly popular.

That's when Monica arrived. She had snuck into his hospital room and promised him fame, money and adoration. Jorge sat impassively until she also promised to take care of all the reporters, phone calls and messages, too.

He was irritated when he was finally released from the hospital to go home a few media types and curious onlookers were still following him. He called Monica and she swore she'd take care of it right away. When he woke up the next morning instead of the 10 or 12 people on his lawn there were dozens, maybe even a hundred.

"What the hell is going on? I thought you were going to take care of this?"

"I know, I was hoping for a better turn out, too, but you just leave it to me."

"But why are they here? I don't want anyone here."

"Oh listen to you all fussy. Here, I made you some coffee. Get dressed; we need to make a statement."

"A what? Do you mean something other than 'get the fuck off my lawn'?"

"Honey, once I work my magic you won't have to worry about it ever again because you'll be in a gated community living next door to Pat Sajak and enjoying the quiet life."

"Pat Sajak?"

"Wear the light blue button up shirt. It makes you look earnest."

The lights were glaring. Teesha was sitting in her mother's lap, fidgeting. The camera adored her with her big saucer brown eyes, haphazard pigtails and obliviousness to how painfully adorable she was. She'd made the cover of People magazine and people from coast to coast ooh'd and ahh'd with each bubbly, innocent utterance.

Jorge was a blurry inset picture on the cover of the Globe proclaiming "Baby Catching Hero Ex-Wife Scandal!" Granted he hadn't paid alimony in six years, but his ex-wife been living with a real estate developer for most of that time. Her gardener made more a year than Jorge so he didn't feel bad about it.

20

Monica told him they were just trying to make him look more human. "Everyone loves kids, but they have to try and tear down adults. If that's the worst they can do then bring it on. The 35-54 male demographic will love you."

The cameraman started a countdown. Jorge shifted uneasily, the lights were already making his head hurt. Teesha was very interested in the buttons on her mother's sleeve.

"Welcome back everyone. By now you've all heard the miraculous story of a little girl—" the camera cut to Teesha for a second "who fell from a fifth story window and survived due to the courageous actions of a total stranger." The camera cut to Jorge who was scratching his nose. Monica gestured frantically for him to stop. The only thing that accomplished was giving him an oddly unsettling expression of confusion and annoyance for the final instant of his cutaway.

"Good morning Shanna, is this little Teesha?" the anchor asked Teesha's mother.

"Yes, yes. She's my little angel," she give Teesha a little squeeze in an attempt to get her to look toward the camera. On the other side of the camera from Monica, the representative for Teesha and her mother was dancing around trying to get her to smile.

"She's beautiful," smiled the anchor. "Can you tell us about that day?"

"Well, I was busy cleaning the bathroom and the cleaners —you know how bad they can smell—they were really bad. So I went into the living room and opened a couple windows to air the place out. I mean, you see Teesha—you see how small she is. I would've never thought in a million years she could have gotten up there.

"I went back to finish cleaning the bathtub. I had the radio on and I didn't know anything until the police came knockin' at my door asking if I'd lost my child." Shanna started tearing up a bit. Her rep gave her a big thumbs up. "I said, 'No officer, my baby's right over there in the living room, playing with her dolls,' but she wasn't there." At that point the tears started flowing. Monica looked enviously over at her counterpart.

"I didn't know what to do because there was no way my baby could've gotten out. I told the officer that she had to be in there."

"When did you find out what had happened?" asked the anchor with deep earnestness. She didn't even have to wear blue, Jorge marveled.

"Well the officer said not to worry, but she'd fallen. I just lost it at that point. I was a-cryin' and wailin'. My neighbor Essy had to come over and calm me down..." her voice cracked. The anchor nodded supportively, either trying to coax more story or more tears—Jorge couldn't decide which.

"I'm sorry. I wasn't going to cry."

The anchor put her hand on Shanna's knee to earnestly show empathy. Shanna wiped away her tears and sniffled quietly before clearing her throat.

"Anyway the officer said the paramedics were just checking her out, but everything seemed okay. It seemed like she was gone forever, but when that ambulance-man brought her up the stairs—it was the best moment of my life."

The anchor broke away and looked at the camera. "What she didn't know was that she had survived because she had been caught by passerby."

The camera cut back to Jorge, who was slouched in the chair, rubbing his temple trying to ease the searing pain in his head. To the television viewing-public, however, he just looked incredibly hung-over.

"What can you tell us about that day?" the anchor asked Jorge.

"Uh, I don't remember that much about it—" from the sides Monica was gesturing frantically, running her hand across her neck trying to get him to stop. She'd worked for hours with him so he'd give the perfect response. It was mostly untrue since he didn't remember "a rush of compassion as Teesha landed in his arms," or "reacting on instinct to protect her."

"Um, I mean I had to catch her 'cuz she was falling. Same as anyone would have done." Monica gave the thumbs up and a triumphant smirk to Teesha's rep. Monica had beaten the "I'm not hero, I just did what anyone would do," line into his head over and over the night before in their prep sessions.

"And how has all this changed your lives?" the anchor asked all of them, but looked at Shanna and Teesha.

They'd actually run through all this before in a sort of pre-interview. Jorge hadn't really paid attention. He knew that he was along for the ride. Everyone wanted to see the cute little kid and watch the mom cry. Cuteness, crying and tits were pretty much the only reasons anyone watched anything anymore it seemed. Two for three wasn't bad, Jorge thought to himself.

"Well there have been so many people who have come forward and been so supportive. I just can't say how grateful we all are about all the gifts and help we've received. It's truly been a blessing."

"And I hear little Teesha's even going to be in a commercial."

"That's right. Someone from Michelin—the tire people—they saw her on the TV and wanted her in one of their commercials."

Jorge snorted and half choked on the water he was sipping. The two women were startled and looked at him.

"I never figured a story like this would end up selling that type of rubber," he muttered.

"What was that?" asked the anchor, unsure if she should be annoyed.

Monica was shaking her head, her face buried in her hand.

"Um, nothing. Just swallowed wrong," said Jorge.

The anchor eyed him, now convinced that she was annoyed. She sat back in her chair and eyed, smiling but her eyes oozed contempt.

"So, how has all this changed your life?" she asked.

"Well, I have headaches."

There was a moment of pause, as if she expected him to say something else. In the pre-interview Jorge had followed Monica's script and answered something about opportunities and wonderful people and some other bullshit.

"Headaches?" she asked, confused.

"Yeah, since the kid smashed my head into the sidewalk I get these headaches. I have seizures sometimes, too. That's why I'm wearing these sunglasses. I'm not a drug dealer."

The anchor's eyes were wide and her mouth hung open dumbfounded. After a second she was able to muster a tentative, "Um."

"I cry a lot now. Sometimes for no reason. I'll just be sitting there and suddenly I'm just bawling and can't stop. Sometimes the only way I can stop is by having a seizure, but that's not so great because when I come to I usually have to change my pants because I pissed myself."

Monica looked like she was going to faint. The more he kept talking, the more at ease Jorge felt. He leaned back in his chair, crossed his legs and sipped his water.

"I'll tell you one thing: the seizures suck and the headaches are horrible, but the worst part is everyone wants to talk about it. But it's never 'Hey man, how are you? You feelin' ok? Are those seizures better?' it's always 'I saw you on TV, what's so-and-so like,' or 'Letterman had a good one about you last night.' And don't even get me started on YouTube. Fuck—"

"And that's all the time we have. Al is next up with the weather," grinned the anchor, teeth shining immaculately and eyes wide in horror.

The cameraman signaled they were off. The anchor and Shanna stared at Jorge with a mix of contempt and revulsion. Jorge didn't notice; he was trying to get a page to get him another bottle of water.

"I hope you're happy," Monica fumed. She grabbed him by the lapel as she dragged him out of the studio. Teesha smiled at him and waved as Monica ushered him into the hall. She really was a cute kid, Jorge thought. He hoped her mom and their publicity person didn't get screw her up too bad trying to make her famous.

Monica shoved him down the hallway towards two men in suits who were chatting with each other. Monica marched up to them, Jorge in tow. The two men didn't so much as look at them as they approached and continued their conversation as if they didn't exist.

"I hear the kid's absolutely adorable," said the first man.

"What about the guy?" asked the other.

"Not much to look at. I hear he's an asshole. Drug dealer, maybe," the first man answered.

Monica's face flushed red, but she stood and smiled as if everything was fine. "Mr. Turner?" she asked.

The first man looked at her disinterestedly. He didn't say anything. There was an awkward silence before Monica launched in on her pitch.

"Mr. Turner, I'm Monica Slawinski, I spoke to your assistant on the phone earlier."

The second man stifled a laugh. He patted Mr. Turner on the shoulder with a smirk; "I'll leave you to it."

"I'll be there in a minute," he answered. Jorge knew that tone. It was the same tone his old foreman used to use when he was about to blow someone off. Monica may have known that, but she never stopped grinning. Her face was returning to its normal hue.

"It was nice to meet you," Monica offered to the second man as we walked down the hallway. He didn't notice.

"Mr. Turner, I know you're busy so I'll only take a moment of your time. I phoned your office about my client." She tugged on Jorge's lapel so he'd come up alongside her. Jorge looked at Mr. Turner and Mr. Turner looked at Jorge. Mr. Turner looked at him like was a smelly old wet dog on new carpet. Jorge looked at him like he was an auditor for the IRS.

"He's been featured on all sorts of news programs. I'm sure you've heard the story—"

"Yeah, I heard a little of the bit they just did on the Today show," he interrupted, clearly hoping that would be the end of it.

"Wasn't it great? Jorge's such a character," Monica laughed a little too loud and abruptly for it to be genuine. "I know you handle a wide variety of clientele and I think with a little polish and your agency behind him he could be a very high-profile addition to your roster—"

"Yeah, I don't think he's right for us. We're moving out of the 'reality' thing right now—"

Monica shooed Jorge down the hallway. "I'll be with you in a second. Business stuff to talk about; it won't be two ticks." Jorge shuffled down the hallway. When she thought he was out of earshot she started in again.

"Listen, he's a prick. I can't stand him. Did you see the Today show thing? It was a disaster. But you know what? *I* got him on the Today show. You think he's more charming outside of here? Do you think he's the eccentric nice guy down the street who collects hubcaps and gives quarters to kids on their birthdays? He's a mess. I'm surprised he didn't kick a kitten in there just to prove he's a piece of shit.

"I got him presentable. I got them to put him on their goddamn show. Think about that—I got the Today show, squeaky-clean, white-bread America to the core, to put him on the air. If you don't think that's turning water into wine I don't know what else to say."

Mr. Turner looked a little surprised, but bemused as Monica continued to hiss through gritted smiling teeth.

"I don't care if you pick him up or not. But your agency needs someone like me. If I can make that… orangutan half-ways presentable, just imagine how I can clean up one of your coked-out little starlets. You need someone like me. Give me a chance and I guarantee it'll be the best decision—" Monica noticed Jorge lingering in the hall. "You go on to the car, dear, I'll be there in a minute!" she called in a cheery sing-song tone.

He headed down the hallway. He heard Monica start in again. He couldn't hear her this time, but the happy sing-song tone was gone and back to the husky, aggressive whisper she had before.

He decided not to go back to the car. Monica had said she had a few more meetings lined up for them later in the day but he was pretty sure those wouldn't go any better than the one they'd just had. It was clear the meetings weren't for him anyway, and given what he'd just heard he was perfectly fine to let Monica look stupid. It was just as well since he hadn't wanted any part of them to begin with. Now he at least had a reason to blow them off.

He found his way to a train station and bought a ticket back to Philadelphia. The ride back was unremarkable. His head still hurt but no one bothered him. He almost felt like a normal person again.

When he got home, rocks had been thrown through his front windows and "FUCKTARD" had been spray-painted across his front door. In all fairness he couldn't really blame the falling child or the Today show for that. It was just as likely it had been done by the dipshits down the street that he'd called the cops on a couple weeks before.

"Home sweet home," he muttered to himself

Once he finished cleaning up the glass and tried scrubbing off the paint he spent the rest of the day working on disability paperwork. Monica had said he wouldn't need to worry about it since she was going to get him some endorsements. Besides the public didn't like heroes on public assistance, she assured him. But the public didn't seem to like him much anyway and it turned out Monica wasn't too interested in finding him endorsements either. Mercifully the media attention had waned but once the appearance of public support vanished the hospital had felt more than safe in sending him strongly worded letters demanding their money. Since he really couldn't work anymore and he wasn't a fan of being homeless he had to fill out the paperwork.

The next few months were difficult. The people at the social security office weren't particularly willing to hand over money and apparently Monica had received payments for a number of appearances on his behalf that she hadn't told him about. When they audited his finances there was a lot of money that he didn't know that he was supposed to be using even though he'd never received it. In the end he received a modest check once a month that helped him keep a small apartment and every other week he could go and pick up some groceries at the food pantry. He didn't grab too much. Usually some powdered milk and eggs, some bread and peanut butter. He thought the better stuff should go to people with kids. He wasn't a nice person, but that didn't mean he was a complete asshole, either, he figured.

One of his few luxuries was grabbing coffee at a café down the street a couple mornings a week. If he was having a good week he even splurged on some hashbrowns.

One morning in the fall a small darker-skinned man came in with a tall thin white man with well-sculpted hair and fingernails that looked prettier than Jorge's ex's. The waitresses were whispering and pointing from behind the counter as the two men settled in.

Jorge's waitress came to re-fill his coffee. At least those were the motions she was mimicking. She had never been really interested in making sure he had enough coffee before and the entire time she was glancing over her shoulder and studying the two men while pouring coffee— mostly on Jorge's hashbrowns.

"You know who that is?" she clacked through her gum.

Jorge shrugged.

"You see that thing about those miners in South America? He's one of those miners. He was trapped in a collapsed mine for, like, two months or something."

Jorge didn't say anything.

"It's just so weird to be around an honest-to-goodness hero," she paused and looked at Jorge. Her expression changed back to the look of irritation and contempt she usually had for him.

Jorge finished reading the section of newspaper he'd swiped from a neighboring table. He left his money on the table and went back to the restroom before heading out. As he was at the urinal the miner came in and took the urinal next to his.

"How's it goin'?" Jorge asked.

The miner smiled and nodded shyly. Jorge wasn't sure if he was being polite or didn't know English.

"They say you're a hero."

The miner looked at him uneasily and shook his head and gestured towards his ear. "No se."

"Yeah, me either," answered Jorge as he finished. He zipped up and went to wash his hands. The miner kept his eyes down, clearly not wanting to chat.

Jorge leaned against the sink as he dried his hands and looked directly at the miner. The minder glanced sideways uneasily, unsure of what to make of the drug dealer that was watching him pee.

"You're the best of right now," Jorge assured him sympathetically as he balled up his used paper towel and tossed it in the direction of the garbage can. The miner looked confused.

"Don't worry; it gets better. Sometimes they give you pills."

The End That Suits You Best

He'd actually fallen asleep.

In his dream he was at his grandmother's house in Montana. In the backyard there had been a cement birdbath surrounded by lilac bushes with an old, crooked apple tree in the back corner looming over all of it.

The air tasted different there. It tasted like being six years old.

The alarm went off. It was the same song as yesterday and the day before. The radio station was one of the few still operating that played music, but whoever had been at the controls had abandoned them days ago. Every morning had a strange déjà-vu feeling about it with the same music playing in the same order day in and day out. Still, it wasn't a bad song—"My Girl" by the Temptations. He liked the bit at the beginning of the chorus that went "Well I guess you'll say, what can make me feel this way?" It sounded so hopeful.

Still only half awake Able rolled over and felt for Lucy. She usually would be curled up behind his knees. He stopped reaching almost immediately remembering that she was gone. He'd had her put to sleep three days ago. A lot of people had been doing it. When he'd gone in it was almost like a factory—they'd walk in a room and walk out almost immediately and then the vet would call another name.

Able knew Dr. Holland from years back—he had been close friends with his parents—so when he'd taken Lucy in Dr. Holland took him into an exam room and did it all properly.

"How you been, Able?" he asked sympathetically.

Able smiled weakly. "Oh, not too bad. Trying to get some things taken care of last minute, same as most people. If I don't get to all of it, it's not like it'll be the end of the world."

They both laughed a little too loudly. Dr. Holland smiled at him as he scratched Lucy at the scruff of her neck.

"It's a terrible business, this," he sighed. "I'm almost glad we're so busy. Keeps the mind from wandering…"

Neither man said anything for a moment. Dr Holland continued to pet Lucy. Lucy ground her head against his palm happily purring. He stopped and let out a tired sigh. "Well, I suppose we should get to it. You sure this is what you want?"

Able nodded. Dr Holland pulled a syringe from his coat and removed the cap. He looked at Able and gave him a little nod. "You're doing Lucy a great kindness. You know that, right?"

Able nodded again, barely able to see through blurred eyes.

It was quick. Lucy didn't even flinch and Dr Holland flipped the needle into his pocket so quickly it was almost as if nothing had really happened. He gave her another pat on the head. Within a couple of seconds she seemed to drift off.

"Do you want to leave her here?"

"No, I'll take her."

Able scooped her up and ran the back of his hand over her head and down her neck.

"You going to be okay?"

"Yeah. I'll be fine."

"Do you have anywhere to go? Any friends or anything?"

"I have to work later."

"That's not what I meant."

Able didn't answer. She still felt warm in his arms. It was better this way. She just fell asleep.

"Thanks doctor. I really appreciate it. I know you're busy —"

"No, no. It's no problem at all. I'm glad I was able to help out. Listen, if there's anything you need…"

"I'll be fine. But if you come by the restaurant I can get you a free dinner. Anything you like, it's on me."

"Well I just might take you up on that, Able. You be careful out there, and good luck to you."

"Thanks. Same to you."

*****

Able poured a bowl of Lucky Charms and sat at the kitchen nook. He'd stayed away from the sweet kids' cereals for years—trying to keep off those extra fifteen pounds that always seemed to find a way through anyway. At this point it didn't seem like it was that important. He'd figured "what the hell" and bought whole milk to go with it. It was like eating dessert for breakfast and it was glorious.

Normally he'd have the TV on to the news while he got ready for work. Now it was all static or color bars or worse, the pre-recorded message that everything was going to be fine. They'd tried to prevent the inevitable panic and

38

it had worked for a while. But how long can you keep the end of the world a secret?

No one would say how long they'd actually known but when the news finally did break it was clear that there was nothing that could be done. Whatever attempts the governments and billionaires had made had failed and they could do nothing to save themselves—no secret bunkers, no space colonies, no Bruce Willis on a rocket ship with a drill. The elites were stuck with the hoi polloi and everyone was going to die. And they'd probably die screaming.

Able cleared off the table and set his bowl in the sink and headed into the bedroom. He put on his work shirt and played with the cheap polyester tie trying to look more grown up than he felt. His cowlick bounced defiantly, intent on making him look like one of those guys who was too clever to take his menial job seriously.

Able had worked at the Hot Plate for nearly eight years. Roger was the owner/manager. Roger spent most of his weekends at the lake getting absolutely hammered. Able had essentially been running the place for the last five years. The food wasn't very good. It was little wonder given what Able had to work with—the cheapest, most suspect, cut-rate ingredients that Roger would begrudgingly pay for. Able had done his best and the restaurant had managed a modest degree of success with a collection of regulars and decent foot traffic most days.

Since the news broke Roger hadn't been at the store more than a couple times. When he was there he was ridiculously drunk. The last time Able had seen him Roger had stumbled out the back service door muttering that he was going to the lake and to call him if he needed anything. That was two weeks ago.

It didn't really matter. Once the news broke, almost no one else came to work. The high school kids barely showed up as it was. The regulars dropped out one by one. The last to go was Marta—she was a 58 year-old single lady from Michigan. She didn't have any family and had taken on the roll of honorary grandmother to the Hot Plate staff. Able had actually been surprised when she hadn't shown up yesterday.

He went by the apartment she had listed on the staff call sheet. When he got there, there was a suicide note taped to the door. Suicides were rampant now. They'd closed the national parks and most major sites and attractions across the country because people were flocking to them to die in a nice place. He really didn't blame them. That's what he'd done for Lucy. It wasn't as if they were going to miss much in the last few days before it all came crashing down.

The note was actually very sweet. She apologized to whoever happened to have to deal with her body and left instructions on her disposal. She thanked everyone she could think of. She had some particularly kind words for Able calling him an "honorable, kind, gentle soul" and said he was like the son she wished she'd had. Able didn't go in. No one would be by to take care of her remains, but it would be over soon enough. It just felt better to Able to let her lie undisturbed.

He wasn't sure what to feel about Marta. He missed her. Part of him felt sad that she felt that she had to commit suicide. Part of him was proud of her for going out on her own terms. In his mind he pictured her both sad and alone as well as strong and brave. He wished he knew which one was right.

Able walked to work. It was a little after 10 when he arrived. The restaurant was supposed to open at six for the breakfast crowd, but since it was just him now he made sure that lunch and dinner were covered. With everyone else gone he had to do all the prep work. Usually if he got in around 10 he'd have everything ready to go by noon.

It actually didn't take as long as it had the last couple of days. He'd gotten down a system for prep. Combined with the realization that things would be slow he didn't actually have too much to do. The last two days he'd ended up throwing a lot out because he'd thought there would actually be customers.

He wrapped up early and had the lights on, the "open" sign turned on and the door unlocked. He looked at the clock and it was only 11:40. He sighed and looked outside—still not a soul to be seen walking around or driving. It was unnaturally silent. He waited a while, but became restless and went into the back to do inventory.

The door chime startled him. He came up and saw a short, skinny guy in his thirties weaving uneasily towards the counter. He reeked of whiskey and when he took off his sunglasses his eyes were wild and glassy.

"Welcome to the Hot Plate, can I take your order?"

The man grinned at him through yellowed teeth. He steadied himself on the counter and pretended to read the menu board.

"Do you still have those little fried things with the ham and the cheese in 'em?"

"I'm sorry, we're all out of ham and cheese bites. Is there something else you'd like?"

"Aw, man. I've been dying for those things. I've been craving 'em for, like, six days. I don't care if they're past date or anything, dude. Dig 'em out of the fucking garbage for all I care. Not like it'll kill me or anything."

"I'm sorry, we're completely out of ham and cheese bites."

"Well... shit."

"Is there something else I can get you?"

"Uhhh..." he wobbled uncertainly as he looked up at the menu again. "Can I get a bacon cheeseburger and some curly fries and.... Oh! Do you have them apple turnovers? I fuckin' love those turnover things!"

"Okay, so that's one bacon cheeseburger, an order of curly fries and an apple turnover. Would you like to add a medium drink and make it a combo for only 20 cents more?"

"Yeah, get me a root beer."

"Alright, your total comes to $8.84," Able handed him a cup and gestured towards the soda fountain. The man looked at him incredulously.

"You're *charging* me?"

"Well, it is the price—"

"Jesus Christ. You afraid you'll get fired if you don't charge?"

Able was confused by the man's outburst. "No, that's not the point."

"Not the point," he mimicked. 'You know what? Fuck it. Here." He threw down a wad of crumpled 50 and 100 dollar bills.

"Sir, I don't have enough to make change for all that," which was true. With the banks closed like most businesses Able didn't have much in the way of petty cash. He had still made the nightly deposits but he'd accidentally shorted himself in the till in the process.

"Just keep the change. It's just paper now, anyway," the man laughed in a squeaky, hiccupy way.

"I can't, it's too much."

"Just keep it. Doesn't matter to me. Doesn't matter to anyone. It's the great reckoning, man. You keep the money. You know why? Because I'm gonna eat my burger and fries and then go out and find the hottest piece of ass, a bottle of jack, a pile of blow and fuck 'til the ground shakes… literally.

"That's the thing. It's up to you. No repercussions. No jobs to go to. No one to tell you it's bad for you because it doesn't fucking matter. You just go out there and find the end that suits you best. It's what we've all been too afraid to hope for and now it's here. Hal-le-fuckin'-lujah! I mean, look at me. You know what I was? I was a fucking real estate agent. I'd sell you a fuckin' three bedroom ranch-style house with a double garage and a goddamn sandox in the back if you wanted. I thought that it was good work. I thought it mattered, but now, shit…"

Able didn't know what to say. The man didn't seem to even be talking to him as much as proclaiming his thoughts to an invisible congregation.

"I'll bring your order out to you when it's ready."

The man was staring at the floor lost in the sermon still echoing in his head. He caught himself and grinned as he wobbled uneasily, "Sounds good, buddy."

Able enjoyed the work. As crazy as the man was, he was the first customer in over a day and there hadn't been more than a couple in the day before that. It was unusual for the place to be open, but even so people didn't seem to be interested in what the Hot Plate had to offer. It was actually nice to be able to work, though. Able gave him an extra large portion of fries. Roger hated it when people did that, but since the place was effectively Able's he didn't feel too bad about it. That and the guy had probably paid $400 or more for the food. It was the least he could do.

He brought the food out to the man who didn't say anything to him. He was on his cell phone talking about "all the pussy" he was going to be getting. He finished and left rather quickly. Given how excitable he had been Able had expected he'd at least say something on the way out of the door but he just left quietly.

Able cleaned the table. He washed the counters… again. He checked that the restrooms were stocked with toilet paper for umpteenth time that day. Once everything had been done, checked and redone probably another four times Able just leaned on the counter by the register and waited. He saw a couple of cars drive by on the street out front, but that was it. He hoped Dr. Holland would come by. Dr. Holland was probably spending time with his family, but Able hoped he'd at least have the chance to get him something to go to show his appreciation. Dr. Holland had been very kind with Lucy. He didn't need to take the extra time, but he did. Such kindnesses should be returned, Able thought to himself.

The sun began to set. Usually Able went and closed the blinds since the front of the building faced west. Customers usually didn't care for being blinded while they were eating, but no one was there. Able watched the sunset behind video rental place across the street and the line of trees that jutted up behind it.

He thought about what the guy earlier had said. This was the end that suited him best, he thought. Well, almost.

About three years ago there had been a dishwasher that worked at the Hot Plate named Ben. He was big and quiet and usually had a scowl. Most of the other staff didn't really like him. He worked there for about a year before he quit and moved to Oklahoma somewhere. Able never really talked with him that much. On breaks they'd sit in the back, Ben would smoke and Able just sat with a soda or iced tea. Able was the only one who would sit with him, though.

Ben lived a few blocks away from Able and they would walk home after work sometimes. On the nights when the moon was new or it was dark and cloudy Ben would let Able hold his hand.

As the sun turned orange and pink Able thought about Ben. He hoped he was okay wherever he was. He hoped he wasn't alone and maybe if he was, he was thinking about those dark nights in October when they walked silently, hand-in-hand down the alley. At the end of the alley their paths would diverge. Able wanted to just stand there a moment longer and sometimes they would.

Ben would always be the first to let go. "See you later," he'd say as he was walking away.

That's what Able wanted to do now. But this is what he had and it was okay. They predicted it was going to happen sometime in the early morning hours. This would be the last time he did the closing checklist. He mopped up the back, wiped and scrubbed the grill. He drained and cleaned the fryer. He cleaned the dining area, restocked the straws and napkins for no other reason than he thought they looked better that way.

When he finished, he surveyed the Hot Plate for one last time. It looked as good as it had looked for as long as he'd worked there. He locked the doors and turned off the lights and grabbed the garbage by the back door. It had been a good day. He'd done his job and left the place in better condition than when he'd first arrived. He'd done a good job—no one could say otherwise.

That would do. That would have to do.

He felt a little sad as closed and locked the back door and tossed the garbage bags into the dumpster.

He walked home, down the alley feeling the gravel shift and pop under his shoes. He wished there had been more. Not more time, just more of everything. But that's how it always goes, he thought to himself. This had been enough.

It had been just enough.

A Dog Named Supper

for Kari

When I asked him why he hadn't said anything—why he didn't tell anyone he just shrugged and said, "I never had a dog before."

As he told it, there was absolutely nothing extraordinary about the dog. He'd picked a little mutt puppy at random within the flurry of ears, noses and tails from a neighbor's litter.

Abner had a well-earned reputation as a recluse. It had been more coincidence that he'd even run into them that day; his old truck had over-heated up by their mailbox. As he waited for it to cool off they'd come home with the puppies they'd been unable to give away at the livestock auction earlier in the day. Abner said the last time he'd seen his neighbor before that was when his neighbor—then a boy of 15—had optimistically walked up to Abner's front door dressed as Frankenstein on Halloween hoping to score a Baby Ruth.

Life on the farm was all Abner had known and he'd had little outside interaction aside from school (which he hated) or church (which he resented). When his father died, Abner had sold off the land except for the farmstead and a couple acres for a garden and parking a couple rusted out old cars. That's where he got his money. People thought he'd amassed a fortune from the stock market or running liquor across the border, but truth was he didn't have much money. He lived cautiously with he did have and often either built or mended what he needed or simply went without. He got some sporadic payments on the mineral rights he retained on the land he had sold so he had been able to sock away some money over the years. In the end it meant Abner didn't have much cause to leave his house and so he usually didn't.

The puppy had been a regular puppy. He chewed table legs, peed on the carpet, chased his tail and smelled everything. He'd shoo birds and gophers in the yard and chase rabbits in his sleep. Everything had been completely normal until, according to Abner, the puppy asked, "Do you smell that too or is just me?"

When he said that I interrupted him and asked him how he had responded: was he surprised? Did he think he was going crazy? What did he do?

"I said I didn't smell it."

"…You just answered him?"

"Well, you asked me a question and I answered you. Seems like the proper thing to do under most circumstances."

*****

"I don't smell anything."

"You sure? It's really… it's kinda like dead gopher and mildew."

"I don't even know what that would be like."

"Really? You seriously can't smell that?"

"You can probably smell better than me."

"That's kind of weird."

"Well, not really. I could always see better than my dad."

"So your nose is broken?"

"I don't think so. I think there's just a difference."

"Well, huh…"

There was a moment of silence as they both contemplated what they could or couldn't do. The puppy leaned sideways and scratched behind his ear with his back foot.

"So… when's supper?" the puppy asked.

"I don't know. Hadn't thought about it yet."

"I'm hungry."

"I guess I can get you some food."

"Yeah, about that—how is it you get to have all sorts of interesting things and I get… what is that stuff? It's crunchy and tastes like poop—I mean I don't mind poop sometimes, but still."

"I don't know. The bag says 'dog food.' I didn't really look into it much beyond that. You didn't really complain or anything."

"Well, I'm going to go on the record and say that whatever it is you eat smells much better than the 'dog food' stuff."

"I suppose it does. I guess I never really paid attention to the smell of your food."

"It's ok. I feel a little bad even mentioning it. It's just some of your food is so interesting. So many smells."

"It's ok I suppose," Abner shrugged. "I'm not a real good cook or anything. I just try and make stuff I like with what I've got around."

"Do you think I could have some?"

"You mean right now?"

"Well, I am hungry, but I was thinking more in general. Nothing much. Just, maybe... one meal a day?" The dog sat looking hopefully up at Abner. The only sound was the swishing of his tail against the floor.

Abner stood looking at the dog for a moment. "Sounds fair. You care which one?"

"Not really. Whatever's easiest," the tail started flopping back and forth exuberantly.

"Ok."

They stood silently on the back steps looking across the open field. The dog squinted contentedly as the breeze blew across his face as he watched the grass sway. Abner tried to inconspicuously see if he could smell whatever the dog had smelled.

"...So what should I call you?"

"My name is Abner."

"And my name is You, right?"

"No. 'You' isn't a name; it's a general sort of thing."

"So what's my name?"

"I hadn't really thought to give you one," Abner confessed. "I barely use mine most the time."

"Can I get one?"

"I suppose. I don't know what to call you, though."

"Well how do you come up with a name?"

"I dunno... You ask a lot of questions, don't you?"

"Well, I've been afraid to ask."

"Really?"

"Yeah, well..." the dog trailed off. Neither said anything for a moment. The dog yawned making a little squeaking noise and then lowered himself down so he was sitting upright looking out over the field.

"...It's not like you talk a lot or anything. You seemed to get annoyed when I made noise before," the dog said after a few minutes.

"That was barking. That's just noise."

"To you maybe. I was just trying to make small talk."

Abner absent-mindedly chewed his thumbnail. He spit out a fragment of nail that had stuck to the tip of his tongue and coughed. "Fair enough. So you want a name..."

The dog's tailed wagged again, making light knocks on the wood of the steps.

"Well, I've never had to name anything before. I guess people are named after someone else sometimes."

"Like who?"

"Family. People they respect. Things like that."

"So who would work for that?"

"Well, my dad's name was Orville."

The dog looked at the ground glumly; his tail stopped wagging. He looked up at Abner who hadn't noticed the dog's disappointment. Abner was still staring at the field thinking he could almost smell something in the breeze.

"Um, I don't know about that one. Can I get a different one?"

"It's your name; make sure it's one you can live with. Lord knows I wouldn't have picked Abner."

"Is there anything else you can get a name from?"

"Well sometimes they use qualities or things they like."

"Supper is my favorite thing."

"Do you want me to call you supper?"

The dog tilted his head in thought for a moment.

"I like Supper."

"Supper it is."

Abner was almost certain he smelled something, then he sneezed. Supper was grinning as he panted quietly. He looked up at Abner and nudged him with his nose.

"…Now I'm *really* hungry."

*****

In our sessions I pressed Abner for more details. He said they really didn't talk that much. He had his things to do and Supper tended to his business, such as it was. Most days they wouldn't say more than a couple words to each other preferring instead to eat silently at their shared meal and then retire to their separate corners of the house.

"How did he learn to speak?"

"Hm? Oh, he said he watched television when I was asleep."

"So did he, um, speak dog too?"

"Of course."

"Weren't you curious what other dogs were saying?"

"Not really."

"Not at all?"

Abner seemed to be distracted by something in his teeth. He contorted his face strangely as he scoured the outside of his teeth with his tongue.

"Abner?"

"Hm?"

"You never asked him about what dogs were saying?"

"I asked him once about a dog on the television."

"What did he say?"

"He said she was a terrible actor."

*****

In their spare time Supper had talked Abner into teaching him to read. Supper wasn't particularly good at it, but was able to get by. Abner said it was probably more his fault since he wasn't all that interested in reading to begin with and probably wasn't the best teacher.

Supper had taken to nosing through whatever books or papers Abner had in the house. Abner didn't like reading so it didn't take long for Supper to go through what little had been lying around. Instead of going to town to find new reading material for Supper, Abner just opened upstairs storage room—it had been his father's bedroom until his death. Afterwards, Abner had kept his parents' things there in big, dusty, unsorted piles. Abner's mother had been a bookworm so there were boxes of books, old magazines, religious tracts and letters stored there. Supper would disappear to the attic for hours at a time, sometimes only coming down long enough to go outside and eat their shared meal.

One summer day Abner was patching a torn-out piece of screen from the front storm door when Supper poked his head around the corner.

"Who's the lady in the picture?"

"Which one?"

"C'mere," Supper led Abner to an old photo album that was opened on the floor. He poked a black and white picture of a woman standing stoically in a long white dress and a large sunhat in a garden.

"That was my mother."

"She doesn't look very happy."

"She really wasn't for the most part. But she really hated having her picture taken too. I'm sure that didn't help."

"Why not?"

"She said she didn't photograph well."

"Hm," Supper paused looking intently at the picture. "You notice how some people say they don't photograph well? Are they worried because they actually don't photograph well or because they do photograph well and they're just ugly?"

"You're saying my mother was ugly?"

"I wouldn't know. You all look more or less the same to me. Some of you definitely smell better than others."

"What about your mother?"

"She smelled ok, I guess."

"No, what about her? Do you remember anything?"

"A little. I was her third favorite."

"I'm sorry."

"No, it was a litter of eight. I was definitely on the right side of things in that respect."

"Ah. Anything else?"

"Well I was really young. I remember she used to clean my ears and that made me happy."

"My mother took me to the Woolworths and she let me share her ice cream sundae."

"I wonder where mine is."

"Mine died seventeen years ago. Cancer."

They found themselves staring at the ground.

"…Well this took a turn, didn't it?" Supper sighed.

"Seems that way."

"I'm going to go outside and paw at something for a while."

"Yeah, I should… yeah."

*****

Abner sat across from me in his pajamas and a robe and hospital-issued flip-flops.

"Good morning Abner. How are you today?"

"About the same as yesterday, I guess."

I pretended to skim my notes. Pretending gave the illusion of thoughtfulness and made me feel a little better about having already made my mind up—at least appearing like I was considering options felt courteous. Besides, my notes were essentially my way of finding different ways of saying the same things over and over again. Truth was Abner wasn't going anywhere. Even if he was cleared to live alone after the stroke there was no way I could give him a psych clearance.

"So last time we were talking about your dog."

"We spend a lot of time talking about Supper."

"Why do you think that is?"

"…You like dogs?"

"Abner, let's start over: dogs can't talk."

"Dogs don't talk."

"Exactly."

"But they can."

"…No."

"Well, I'd know better than you."

"Abner, there was no dog."

"If you say so."

I was hoping to rattle him, or at least make him question what he was here for. He just seemed bored.

"When the police arrived there was no dog."

"He was gone by then."

"Ok, where did he go?"

"I'm not sure. It was up to him."

*****

"I'm not one to say anything, but you don't look good."

Abner sat slouched, pale and sweating in his recliner.

"I don't feel very well. I don't think I'll be able to make lunch for us."

Supper laid down on the circular rug in the middle of the living room facing Abner.

"Are you old?"

Abner's eyes opened like they were coated in wallpaper glue.

"I suppose I am."

"What's old for you?"

"I feel really old now," Abner let out a half groan half sigh. "It's hard to say. Old always seemed about ten years from where I was. Then at one point I'd passed it and I was old. But I always feel like I'm only a year or so into old, even though I've been old for at least ten years."

"That seems complicated."

"It is to explain it, but it's pretty straightforward when it's happening."

"I'm not old, am I?"

"Well it's different for you. You're about five years old. Depending on how things work out you're not quite halfway through. I don't know what it's like to be a dog, so I don't know when you'd start to feel old. It shouldn't be for a while though."

"I feel normal."

"It's like that most of the time. When you don't feel normal is when you're old."

"What does that mean?"

"It means you don't have to worry about it."

"That doesn't really help."

"Sorry."

"Now I'm afraid I'm going to die."

"…Christ."

Supper's tail started flapping buoyantly as he gave what could be most closely described as a wry grin. "I'm kidding."

Abner looked at him incredulously and then shook his head. "Pretty proud of yourself, aren't you?"

"A little."

"You should take it on the road."

"How do you mean?"

"It's an expression. It's like saying you should do something for a living. But a lot of times it's said sarcastically."

"I bet I could."

"Could what?"

"Do it for a living."

"You want to be a comedian?"

"Well, maybe. I was thinking more just talking. There are people on the television who talk about all sorts of stuff all day."

"Like actors on shows?"

"No, the people who tell you about things. You usually don't see them, but they talk about how tasty Raisin Bran is or how a knife can cut through a brick and then cut a tomato with sleek precision."

Abner didn't move for a moment. Supper wondered if he'd drifted off to sleep but then Abner's eyes opened a sliver and his clear blue eyes appeared between mattery eyelids.

"I think you'd probably do well at that. You've got a good voice."

"I practice sometimes when I'm alone."

"How do you practice?"

"I just do the stuff from the TV, but I do it better. I try to make it sound more interesting."

"Hm."

"I think I'm getting pretty good. Here, let me show you."

Supper sat up, straightened his back so he was sitting at full attention looking very official. He cleared his throat and then paused for a moment before locking his eyes onto Abner's.

"Are you tired of your lettuce going limp? Bothered by withered broccoli? Do rotten apples make you irate? Then you need the Wonder Bag—just slip your favorite fresh fruits or vegetables inside and keep them fresher longer.

"We put this head of cauliflower in the Wonder Bag and this one in the leading plastic zip bag. Look, after a week the one in the old zipper bag is already is wilted and moldy, but the cauliflower in the Wonder Bag is still crisp and fresh even one, two, THREE weeks later!

"Other produce bags can go for as much as $59, but if you act now you'll get the Wonder Bag for only $19.95 plus shipping and handling. If you act in the next 20 minutes we'll double your order for *free*.   Just pay additional shipping and handling charges.

"But wait, there's more: we'll also include the Perfect Egg Maker that allows you to make perfect hard boiled, poached, scrambled or fried eggs every time absolutely free. Hurry, this offer won't last long. Order now and get two Wonder Bags and the Perfect Egg Maker for the low, low price of $19.95. Call now!"

Supper sat perfectly still, watching Abner for any expression. There was a moment of silence.

"Jesus."

"Did I do okay?"

"I don't think you took a breath for that whole thing."

"Well, I want to try to make it sound as official as I can."

"You certainly did that."

"So it was good?"

"I want to buy one of those bags now."

Supper laughed and flopped back to the floor. "I made it up. You can make up anything as long as you say it the right way—it has to sound like it can do anything."

"I knew there was a reason I didn't like the TV." Abner shifted in the recliner so he was facing Supper more directly. "Well, you did one hell of a job. I think you could definitely be one of those TV guys if you wanted."

Supper didn't say anything but his tail danced around whacking the floor with forceful irregular knocks.

"I need to rest for a while. You going to be ok?"

"Yeah, I think I'll go outside and roll around in stuff for awhile. Maybe dig a hole while I'm at it."

"Wake me up when you want something to eat."

"Ok. Get some rest."

*****

"So that's right before you came to us?"

Abner watched a bird on the windowsill before realizing I had said something.

"What? No, no. That was months ago."

"So you were having symptoms that far back?"

"No, I just had the flu."

I jotted down a quick note. It appeared Abner had lost his sense of time and was still easily confused when chronologically ordering events. "Ok Abner, but we were talking about where your dog is."

"I know. I was getting to that."

"So where is your dog?"

"I told you I don't know. I was sick and Supper woke me up later to get something to eat."

"…And?"

"He asked me what would happen if anything happened to me."

*****

"So if I die, what will happen?"

"What do you mean?"

"What would you do?"

"I'd probably bury you in the back."

"Would you get another dog?"

"Why all the questions?"

"Well, talking about getting old and you being sick just made me think."

"About if I'll get another dog?"

"Yeah. That and what happens when you die. What you'd do if I died. What would happen to me if you died."

Abner stirred the beans and franks he had simmering, thinking.

"I don't think I'd get another dog."

Supper came up to Abner and sat next to him. Abner absent-mindedly scratched behind his ears.

"I don't know what happens when we die. Some people say that's it; you're just dead. Some people say you go to heaven or hell. Some people say you do it all over again."

"Which one do you like the most?"

"Well it's not the one where you do it all over again. Once has been plenty for me. I think I'd rather that it would just be it. Seems like there's no pressure there, no reason to get bent out of shape if someone disagrees with you."

"I think I like heaven and hell."

"Why's that?"

"It just seems like things balance out that way. I like thinking that regardless of how things turn out, in the end there will be a reckoning."

"You sound like my dad."

"Really?"

"Yeah. He was all about the fire and brimstone and judgment stuff. I always watched him and wondered if he would end up on the side he thought he would. I guess I just decided that it wasn't worth the bother... Want some beans?"

"Yes please."

Abner served up a couple scoops of beans and franks on a plate. He set it gingerly on the floor. Supper waited until Abner had served himself and sat at the kitchen counter. Abner was still feeling ill so he mostly poked at his food and pushed it around his plate. Supper on the other hand quietly lapped up the beans and licked his plate clean.

"If I die you should leave. I've got some money in an old coffee can underneath the porch. It's yours. I don't know what you want to do. You could do that voice thing if you want to. I think you'd be good."

"You want me to leave?"

"I think you should do whatever you'd like. But if you stay I think you'll end up in the pound or chained to a clothesline alongside a trailer or something. I think you'd be better making your own way. You'd probably do better than most people I've met."

"I don't want to go."

"Well, I don't want to die so I think we're both covered at this point."

*****

"Abner, can I tell you what I think?"

Abner had been looking back out the window again and really didn't seem to be paying me that much attention.

"Sure."

"It sounds to me that you've constructed a very elaborate fantasy. You say you have a dog that talks, but no one's seen him. You say that's because he's off doing commercials. They can't find a food dish or evidence of having a dog. You say it's because he acts like a person and eats your food.

"Every time someone asks you about why there's no evidence you create a more involved layer to the story. I am going to tell you that I think you need to start treatment for schizophrenia on top of your rehabilitation from your stroke. Do you understand?"

Abner sighed but didn't turn to look at me. "Look, I know you guys aren't going to let me go home again. I'm old, I can barely walk and I still can't work my left side worth a damn. I can't dress myself and I have seizures—and that's just the stuff I can remember that's broke. You'd be crazy to let me go.

"I don't care if you think I'm crazy, but could you just let me alone? Save your poking and prodding for someone who would actually appreciate it."

I looked at Abner. It was the first time he had asked for anything and he hadn't pleaded but just sounded tired and frustrated.

"So does that mean you acknowledge that the story you're telling me might not be true?"

"I'm saying that I did have a dog but I know no matter what I say you won't believe me. I'm saying that I can't prove it, and even if I could I wouldn't want to..." Abner's voice trailed off. After a moment he spoke again, his voice softer, "Supper was a good dog but he's off doing what he wants now. I wouldn't be much good to him like this anyway. He doesn't need to be worrying about me. You guys are taking all my money anyway so you might as well be the ones that have to change my underpants when I can't control myself.

"You've got kids, right doc? Would you want them tied to you if you were in my position? Or would you want them doing the things they should be doing? And Supper's a dog. We both know they don't live all that long. He shouldn't spend his time around here. I gave him what I could and I hope it helped.

"I know you got to fill out your papers and make your reports but could you just let it be? Let me eat jello and sit in the dayroom and pretend like I'm playing bingo with everyone else. I won't cause you any trouble. I can't go anywhere; I never hurt anyone. I'm sorry if I'm a pain in the ass, but I'm not used to all the people about. Just give me a little corner and you won't hear a peep from me. I'm sure I don't have that much time left, anyway... Just let it be."

I wasn't able to grant his request, but I did try to keep his medications to a minimum. I'll say this for old Abner: he never changed his story. But he did resist talking about the dog after that. He did keep true to his word, though. He never caused a fuss, even when he was wheeled into group activities he had no desire to participate in or when the hospital served Mexican—he clearly didn't care for the hospital burritos. Can't say I blame him on that one. I would've said something if I were him.

Some of my patients who have had strokes hang on and fight back. They could go for years, decades even. But you could usually tell which ones were going to fight tooth and nail. Abner wasn't one of those. He always seemed cognizant, which, given his illness and schizophrenia, was a bit of a marvel. But he seemed content that he'd had his time. When he came down with pneumonia a few months later, he went quickly and quietly.

Truth be told, I kind of missed him. He was a character, but a good soul. He was good with a quip and was unapologetically frank.

...Ok, this is silly but I have to say this just because it stands out in my mind. I'm sure it doesn't mean anything but I'll always remember this when I think of Abner: Abner never really smiled much. He didn't usually show much emotion at all, but there was one thing that always made him smile and it was the strangest thing.

Every time that commercial for that produce bag came on —you know the one, the "I can't believe the cauliflower is still crisp" one—he would beam. It was strange. I guess you can never tell what random thing can comfort someone who's mentally ill like that, but I'm glad whatever he saw or heard made him happy.

The Icicle Tree

Owen

The girls look beautiful. Sarah's hair is dancing haphazardly in the wind and she has to constantly brush it out of her eyes. Tabitha's had been cut shorter since I'd last seen her. She's wearing a black Alice band that keeps her hair more in place than Tabby's. They're huddled together in their black dresses. They're standing so close to each other but they seem miles apart. Tabitha is crying. Sarah is just standing there, face ashen and stony with a stare that's looking a thousand miles away.

Sarah has to be by eight now. Tabitha is five, but her birthday is in three weeks, I remember that. They grow up so fast. They look more and more like her every day.

I know I shouldn't have come. I hoped maybe it had all been a mistake and that she was actually fine, or that seeing the casket about to be lowered would help it hurt less.

Maybe part of me was hoping that I wouldn't feel anything at all.

I can't stay long. I just have to keep walking. My leg is aching. I'm trying not to limp. They might notice me if I walk like me. My hand is locked in my pocket, which helps keep me look less obvious, but it's harder to balance.

I steal another glance. I can barely see them. I got this far without crying but now I can't stop. There's an enclosed bus stop ahead. I hope I can make it. My body doesn't want to move anymore. I just want to stop, sit down right in middle of the sidewalk and never get up again.

Myrna

I don't know what to think anymore. He's a grown man. I know this. I understand he needs to be independent.

Let me start again.

We were happy that he was healthy. We'd lost two before him, so even when the doctor told us about the damage we were happy. We were scared and we wanted things to be good for him, you know? But we couldn't have loved him more. We didn't wish for him to be any different than he was—he was perfect; he was our son. We'd waited so long for him and even the news about his condition couldn't keep us from being happy.

When you're a mother you learn how to care for and protect your child. Once you've got that down it seems like you have to learn to love at a distance and to just let some things happen—even if it breaks your heart to just stand by and watch. But what other mothers don't understand is how much more... I don't know what the word is—it's so much bigger when you have a child with a disability.

And Owen, he's not even disabled. At least not in the way I think of. He wasn't in a wheelchair. He was incredibly bright. He just had a hard time getting around.

I was in a support group with other mothers whose children couldn't walk, couldn't speak and I don't know how they do it. They're really amazing women. They're amazing mothers. So I'm not complaining and I'm not comparing Owen to anyone. But for me, in my heart, I knew things would be harder for him. I had to help him be stronger and show him that those things didn't matter—not in a real way.

Here's the best way I can describe it—when Owen was in first grade there were some steps that kids had to use to get to and from the playground. There was a separate handicapped access ramp around the side of the building, but the steps themselves were just steps. Owen refused to use the ramp. Kids would make fun of him for being so slow. He'd trip sometimes and he'd get scraped and bruised and the kids would make fun of him for that. I don't think he dared use the ramp even if he'd needed it because of the teasing.

Finally I couldn't take it anymore—he'd come home crying every day for a week. He'd be so angry at himself for not being like the other kids—I think that was as bad as the teasing, really. I had to do *something*. We had steps at home and Owen handled them just fine, but he'd always use the handrail. When I dropped him off at school I realized that was it—there was no handrail or support for those steps.

I went to the principal and asked them to install a handrail. When that didn't do it, I went to the superintendant. I went to the PTA. I went to the school board. And then I started all over again.

I'll be damned if by that next spring I hadn't gotten that handrail installed. I felt like I'd accomplished something. It wasn't a big thing, but it was a little something that would make his life easier. I admit I was proud of myself, so much so that the day after it was installed I waited across the street in the car to see how it went.

The kids came running out for recess. A lot of them used the handrail—some hung on it, a couple tried to slide down it but most of them used it properly. But the point was they used it; it was a "normal" thing. Owen was the last one out with his stiff little limp. He came to the steps and I was so excited. And he limped down the middle of the steps, not even looking at the handrail.

I'd tried to protect him and he wouldn't have it. I was crying in the car. I was a little embarrassed, but mostly I was proud. I was embarrassed because I felt like I should have known better—I should have understood Owen. And I was proud because he was determined to be bigger than what others thought he could do. He wanted to be better than what the other kids thought he could be.

That's what it's like. It's heartbreaking and amazing and each day you learn how to be a better person. Or at least you learn how to be patient.

So when he moved out I knew he had to do it. But I couldn't help but worry.

That's what we do; it's our job.

Micah

Mom is doing the dishes. Most of the visitors have left. Tabby is asleep in her room. She cried herself to sleep again. Sarah is the one I worry about most. She's hardly cried at all. She's tried to be the responsible adult—trying to help coordinate the reception, getting people seats, letting them know where the food was.

Mom has let her do a lot of it. She says it's good if Sarah keeps busy. Some kids just need that, I guess. I don't know what to think.

I ought to do something. But every time I try, I just wonder what she would have done. She took care of the girls. She knew what they should wear. She knew what songs they liked listening to in the car. She knew what their favorite foods were.

I miss my wife. I miss my best friend. I miss you, Miriam.

I haven't been able to keep any food down for the last four days. Mom says I look thin. I just dismiss it. She doesn't need to know. She's got enough to worry about with the arrangements and helping with the girls.

Dad hasn't said much. I don't think he knows what to do. It's probably the most honest response that anyone has given me.

And then I think: I'm glad this didn't happen three months ago. I feel disgusted that I think that. Things weren't good then. But she came back to me. To me. She chose me and our life and our girls. If this had happened before... I might have been glad. What kind of person does that make me?

And every time I'm about to crack and I think I'm going to start crying and never stop something pops into my mind. It's always something different, but it makes me remember something beautiful about her. They're just little snapshots of moments: how she'd say something in a tone of voice that let you know she really wanted something else, the way she would tilt her head when she was really listening to someone, her dorky little snort-laugh that embarrassed the hell out of her, or that sly look she'd give when she wanted to fuck.

It's horrible and brilliant all at once. It's like those memories bring me back from the edge, but then the next moment they make me feel like I've just lost her all over again.

What am I going to do?

Mr. Patel

Goddammit, where the hell is the broom? I tell Owen, "Go sweep the back," and he disappears. I think he's gone to sweep, but no, he's nowhere. It's just as bad as it was before, but now I don't even have a broom.

I don't get involved in my employees' personal lives. I pay minimum wage, so I have to settle with who I get and be glad if they don't steal. Owen doesn't steal but you never know what he's going to be like.

I hire him and he's this quiet, shy kid. He's got the limp and the one arm that don't work so good, but I don't care. Last guy sold pot to school kids when I wasn't around. Piece of shit. So Owen applied and seemed like a good kid —a little old for this kind of work, but I'll take a good worker. It's not my business why he's doing this kind of work, but like I say, I don't get into any of that.

He was a good worker. Never said much to start with, but about six months in he started to get chattier. Not in an annoying way, but just kind of friendly. So I get to know a little about him and he starts to warm up to customers. It was good.

Now I don't know much about him. I don't think he was much with the girls—the limp and stuff. Girls don't like crippled boys like that. I told him once that they wouldn't notice so much if he just stood up straight and tried to look normal. He was a nice boy. He probably wouldn't get a pretty girl, but he could at least get a nice girl.

Out of the blue he starts being extra happy. My nephew Vijay—he runs the counter most days—Vijay says that Owen has a girl now. I think this is good. I am happy for him, I really am. But now he daydreams and is on the phone a lot. Nothing too bad. He couldn't be any worse than Vijay. But still doesn't work as hard as he did, you know?

Then a few months later Owen calls in sick—every day for a week! I don't think much of it the first few days, but he hardly ever calls in sick. He said before he couldn't afford to be sick. I guess he just has a little apartment. I guess if it were bigger I'd know he was stealing or selling drugs because I don't pay him much. Heh.

I was about to put up the "help wanted" sign again since I was sure wasn't coming back and then he just appears one day. But he looks terrible. I thought he was coming off drugs or something. I caught him in the cooler crying. I ask Vijay what's going on and he says that something happened with Owen's girl—that she won't talk to him anymore.

Well, I was a young man once; I know how things can be. I would've never cried in the cooler, but it can be tough. So I give him some room. I figure in a couple weeks everything will be good. But he stayed the same.

Well, he did get a little better—no more crying at least, but still absent-minded and sulky. Then four days ago, it's like he just snapped. Crying in the cooler again. I think he was throwing up. I asked everyone if he was drinking or on drugs or something but they say no. No one knows what's wrong with him. I finally had enough and told him yesterday that he needed to straighten up or find another job. I hired him to clean floors not to cry or scare off customers.

He just kept saying "Sorry, Mr. Patel," over and over. But his eyes, they don't change. His eyes look dead. Very strange.

So I give him one last chance. And he seemed to be getting by. Until now.

Where the fuck is my broom?

Owen

I threw up twice at the bus stop. I couldn't go back to work. The caller ID said Mr. Patel called six times. He's probably going to fire me. It doesn't matter anymore. He should fire me. I'm no good for anyone.

Whenever I close my eyes I see her. Every time I fall asleep I dream of her. Sometimes they're of her leaving me again. It's worse when I dream of us when we were happy —when she was happy with me. Thinking of how we were happy just makes me hate myself more.

There's nowhere I can go that doesn't remind me of her.

I remember the first time. I didn't expect it. I don't even know how it happened. We were flirting I guess. I thought I was just being silly. Girls don't like me. Especially married ones with husbands who can walk straight and have good jobs.

I'd never really been with anyone before. She was so soft. It wasn't even full sex. She touched me, but she wasn't disgusted by leg or my arm. She held my bad hand, all rigid and bent, and pressed it to her breast as she kissed me.

I've never felt like what normal people feel like. They always look at me different. And even if they don't, I know it's because they don't bother to think of me at all. I don't matter to anyone. I'm just a cripple that walks funny.

But with her it felt like that it could all be different. It was like my problems didn't matter at all to her—she didn't even see them. No, that's not it. She saw them, but she loved me more—not out of pity, but because she believed they made me better. I don't know how else to explain it. She made me believe that I could have something good and it could just be good—no caveats, no exceptions.

She put her mouth on me and she looked so happy as she massaged it with her tongue. She looked at me as she sucked it. "I like that I do that to you," she whispered as she held it in her hand. "I like that I make you hard."

I came in her mouth and she held it there until I finished. I always heard the girls at work say how they didn't like the taste but she swallowed it and then licked up the little that was left over. She smiled at me when she finished.

She let me touch her next. She showed me how to do it. Her back arched and she gasped and she put her hand on my cheek when it happened. She looked at me, face flushed and smiled with a dizzy happy look and whispered "Oh, wow."

I held her and we didn't say anything for a while. She was lying on her side, back to me. My good hand was on her stomach, my other was around her shoulder, where she reached up and clasped my hand.

"This can never happen again," she said finally.

"I know."

"I love Micah"

"I know."

"…I'd never do anything to hurt him."

"It's ok."

I thought she was going to leave, but she just held my hand more tightly.

"When I was in college I had never been on my own before. Micah was up at State and I only got to see him every couple of weeks. I didn't know what I was doing.

"I met a guy at a party and he took me back to his place. He didn't even care about me. He just fucked me. When he finished he rolled off of me and told me to get out.

"The worst part of it was I went back two more times. He was rough with me. It hurt. But I went back. It made me feel worthless but I went back...

"...I've never told anyone that before."

"Thank you for telling me."

She kissed my hand. "I trust you. I think I trust you more than I've ever trusted anyone else."

Those are the memories that haunt me. It wasn't the sex, although that was part of it. It was being important to someone. She didn't need me. She had her perfect husband. But she chose me. She wanted me.

But that's gone now. She's gone now. No one chooses a freak forever. I should be glad that I was happy for a little while. But remembering what it felt like is its own hell.

Myrna

It was time for him to go. I know it, but it wasn't as if we thought he was a burden. He had his room in the basement. He had his own door to come and go as he pleased. He made most of his own meals down there. It really was like his own little apartment. But I guess being "like" an apartment isn't the same as actually having his own apartment.

I didn't know how he was going to make it. He did his volunteer work at the Center and he worked at the convenience store for Mr. Patel. He wasn't exactly making a lot of money. But Burt—that's his father—said to just let it be.

I know he's a smart, responsible man, but I'd like it if he wasn't living paycheck to paycheck. He finished his degree; he could have found something in his field. Or gone to grad school. But once he finished school he didn't seem that interested in doing that anymore. I mean it's fine, but I'd hoped he'd find a nice job and settle down. Maybe meet a nice girl. I guess that's what most mothers want.

It was strange having him live somewhere else. It really felt like suddenly he had this entirely different life that we were intruding in on. I think it just felt like that we weren't invited to whatever he was doing. He said he never had anyone over so I guess it wasn't as if he was doing all sorts of things we didn't know about. It just made him seem further away.

When he still lived with us I knew there were times when he'd get down—I could tell by the music playing or how he looked coming and going. So I'd make him a little something special for dinner and run it down to him or have him come up to play cards or watch a movie with us. He didn't always seem very thrilled with it, but it helped get him out of his hole for a while. I don't know who's going to get him out now. I don't know who's watching out for him.

There have been times I've called and I knew he was there, but he didn't pick up the phone. I told myself he was probably busy or in the bathroom or something, but I worry. And it hurts, I can't say otherwise. I can't be that bad, can I? Sometimes I think he wouldn't leave at all if it were up to him. I just wish he had more friends.

He did have a nice friend at the Center. Nice married girl. I never met her, but my good friend Liza knows her. She said she's really sweet. I hoped maybe her and her husband would take him in—have him over for a barbeque during the summer. Something nice like that. I think if Owen had some friends who did normal friendly things with him he might try and be a bit more social.

Anyway, I don't know if he still talks to her. The Center called and said he hadn't been there in over a month. I tried calling him, but no answer... again. I even went by his apartment. I made him some brownies. I heard him moving around inside, but when I knocked he didn't come to the door. I called his father on my cell phone and he told me not to worry—to let him have his space. I left the brownies there, but it didn't feel right. It still doesn't.

I came back the next day and the plate was still there, pushed to the side so it wasn't blocking the door anymore. I wrote him a note and pushed it under the door. I just wanted him to call me. I want to know he's alright.

I feel like he's treating me like a stranger. But I'm not. I know him better than just about anyone else. I just wish he'd talk to us. I feel like he's in some sort of trouble, but no one seems to know anything.

I went by his work. I pretended like it was just a coincidence that I happened to be in the neighborhood and needed some milk, but he wasn't there. The boy behind the counter said he hadn't seen him for a couple of days. Then his boss, Mr. Patel came up from the back. He was very polite, but he said he didn't know anything either. He told me if I talked to Owen to ask about a broom.

I don't know what that means, but I'm worried. I haven't been sleeping well. I feel like there's something I should do. I feel like I deserve at least an explanation or for him to pick up the phone. Just pick up the phone for a minute and say he's alive.

That's not asking so much, is it?

Micah

Gerald and Gloria, Miriam's parents, took the girls for the afternoon. Mom and Gloria started sorting through her things. They try to do it covertly so I won't notice. I think they're trying to spare me from having to think about it.

Part of me hates them for touching her things—for presuming that somehow the fact her shirts aren't in the closet anymore means I will miss her less. Or maybe that with fewer reminders that I won't see her everywhere I go or hear the deafening silence where her voice used to be.

The other part of me wants to burn the house down. If I can't be with her I want every trace of her wiped off the face of the Earth. Living as if she never existed has to be easier than living without her.

I've been doing thank you notes. They're mechanical —"Thank you for your (flowers, card, memoriam, casserole—circle as many as apply). We appreciate your/your family's sympathy and support during this difficult time. Miriam touched us all in a very special way blah blah blah. Sincerely, the Leftovers."

I don't have to think too much while doing them, but just enough to where it's hard to let my mind wander.

I was supposed to go fishing with Millsy and Cooner this weekend. We had a two week trip scheduled since March. I suppose I'll have to watch the girls now instead. I lose my wife and then I lose my life. To say that it's unfair doesn't even cover it. This isn't the life I wanted. This isn't the life we planned for. Fuck.

It just builds in my stomach and I can't believe that a God or the universe could just shit on us like that. We're good people. We don't cause trouble. We give to charity. We don't deserve this. She didn't deserve to die. I don't deserve to be a single parent. We had plans.

I wasn't supposed to have to do this alone.

Owen

I didn't think too much about her when we first met. She was nice and funny but, I don't know, she didn't really catch my eye. We worked together at the Center. She'd been volunteering longer than I had, but she did more administrative stuff. I did clean-up and helped in the kitchen. Our paths really didn't cross until she covered for Phyllis after Phyllis had her back surgery.

Looking back on it, I can't believe I didn't see how amazing and beautiful she was right away. But I didn't and we just had fun. She was really kind to me. She didn't ever say anything about my limp or my arm. She just talked to me like I was a person.

We joked around. She told me about the girls and how her weekend was. It sounds too simple when I try to describe it: she told me about her family and where she grew up— she just kind of told me anything and everything. She was funny and smart and she liked me. I mean she may have *liked* me then, but I didn't know. I just know she liked telling me about what was going on with her and she liked hearing what I had to say.

She was curious about what I studied in college and was always going on about how smart I was. I wasn't trying to show off, but she always would make it sound like I was saying something really deep or interesting. It made me feel important. I liked being around her.

We flirted a bit from time to time. It wasn't serious. How could anyone take flirting from me seriously? We'd joke about making out or I'd make a comment about her top— usually starting out innocently but she'd take it and run with it. We'd just laugh about it in the end.

I didn't even notice that things had changed. But after she left and I was alone cleaning she sent me a text, "When did we go from friendly to flirtatious?"

I thought she was mad at me—that I'd crossed a line so I apologized. She replied, "Not what I meant. It just seems like it's gone further."

"I don't know. It's been fun."

She didn't reply right away. I thought the matter was put to rest, but then I got a surprise. "Have you ever thought of me when you've done it?"

"I don't know what you mean." It wasn't a lie because she couldn't mean *that*.

"Don't be coy."

I had a couple of times, but she wasn't a regular in my imagination. "Yes. You?"

"Yes. A lot lately."

My heart was pounding. I didn't know what to think, but it was like a different part of me took over. "Are you doing it now?"

"OMG NO! The girls are in the other room."

"Are you wet?"

There was a delay in the response. I was sure she wasn't going to answer me…maybe ever again. Then:

"Yes. I've never seen this side of you before."

"Can you be quiet? You should do it now."

"OK. But I have to be quick."

That's how it all started. I felt powerful. I was able to get her to do what I wanted. I felt like I was like a normal guy. I felt better than a normal guy because even with my arm and leg I was able to make her want to get off thinking about me. I'd never felt anything like it before.

When we finished our exchange—it went on for a while—I felt a little guilty. I thought I'd taken advantage of her and that if she'd been in her right mind she would have never done that with me. I figured that would be the end of it. I vowed that would be the end of it. I thought it would just be uncomfortable for her if I said anything. There was no way she couldn't regret it once the dust settled.

The next day I didn't really see her. I felt sad, but it was the way it had to be. I couldn't make her happy. I was a mistake and the sooner she was able to forget about it, the better. She saw me on her way out and gave a little wave. It felt like she was being polite.

Two minutes later my phone chimed with a message.

"You make me feel so beautiful."

My hands were trembling. I'd never felt so alive. It was electric.

Micah

Gloria has been here the last couple weeks. We've been settling in to a schedule. The routine helps.

Gloria takes the girls to swimming on Tuesdays and Thursdays and to the library on Fridays. She helps keep the house up. School is starting in six weeks and then they'll be busy with that.

I'm glad to be back at work. The first few days were hard —I dialed her cell phone once to see if she needed anything at the store on my way home just out of habit. The guys have been good. It's been nice to be able to grab lunch with them and joke around at the office. It's the one place that she doesn't seem to be everywhere.

Tabby still wakes up crying a lot. So do I, if I'm being honest. But it helps to be able to talk to her and help her feel better. We talk about Miriam. Tabby tells me about the things she remembers: how Miriam used to sing her to sleep, how she used to make pancakes in the shape of Mickey Mouse's head and about the times when she'd take her to the grocery store.

I remember things like that too—how she'd laugh giddy and unhinged when she had a bit too much to drink, how she smelled after a day of working at the Center, how she smiled when she thought no one was watching. I still remember when we first met. We were high school sweethearts; she was a sophomore and I was a senior. I think she'd decided on me before we even started going out.   She was like that.   If something caught her imagination she was unstoppable.

Maybe that was part of the trouble.   The girls never knew about it.   She swore he'd never been to the house or met them.   Even now when I want to remember the beautiful things about her, I still remember that.   Things could have been perfect.   But now's there's this shadow over all our memories.

Sarah has become more withdrawn.   Gloria says she's heard her crying when she thinks no one's around.   Whenever I get home she's always busy trying to help her grandmother with supper or fussing over chores.   I suppose she's my daughter in that respect.   Tabby always seemed to have more in common with her mother.

I just don't know what I can do for Sarah.   I don't know that it will be alright.   I don't know if I can forgive Miriam for not being here.   I don't know if I can forget there was someone else.

Mr. Patel

Vijay says I need to do something.   He's probably right, but Owen, he's a good boy.   He doesn't have anywhere else and he used to be a good worker.

Some guys they stop being good workers because they're lazy or smoking dope or stealing.   That's not Owen.   I think he could be a good worker again too—he's not a bum, but he needs to get his head right.   He still cries in the cooler.

Vijay thinks it's still about the girl. He said she died a few weeks ago. She leaves him and he's sad. She dies and he's even more sad. I say if some girl leaves me like that, I wouldn't be so upset if she dies. My wife, she's says I'm bad for saying such things but I just say what I think.

It must be tough for him with his problems, but he should move on. Girls come in to the store and they tell Vijay that they think he's creepy. Girls might not like crippled boys so much, but they really don't like creepy boys.

The other day Vijay had enough and told me I had to talk to him. I went to find him and he was in the back alley just sitting on a milk crate staring at the ground. I don't know how long he'd been out there, but it had been a while if Vijay was complaining about it.

"Owen, why am I paying you if you never work?" I ask him. I yell at him a little. I'm not really mad at him, but he doesn't react. You yell at most people they get mad or scared. They yell back or they apologize—that's how people work. But he doesn't move. He just mumbles "Okay, Mr. Patel. It won't happen again," over and over again. I wish he was on the drugs because then it wouldn't be so strange.

I tell the wife that I worry about him and she says to me, "You can't be so soft! Your job isn't to fix Owen. Your job is to run the business. He's no good anymore. You need to get rid of him."

She used to really like Owen. I think maybe she still does and that's why she doesn't like seeing him around like that.

It's like watching a pet die. You just want to put it to sleep at some point.

Maybe I am getting soft, but I've run my store for 37 years. It's still open. We still have money. We've survived eight robberies, a fire and I don't know how many different employees—some good, most not so good. I think giving Owen a little more time won't sink us.

But I would like to know where he takes that broom. It disappears with him, but always reappears. Very strange. If he wants to steal the broom, just steal it. Running off with it is just odd.

Myrna

I called Owen's friend, Liam, the other day. They spent time together in college and I know they used to get together to go the movies and things like that. Owen never had a lot of friends, but he usually had good friends. You know—the type of friends that would check up on him, always return calls, just really solid, decent people. I always thought that spoke well of Owen, that he surrounded himself with good people.

Liam was surprised but polite. He said he hadn't heard from Owen in a few months. He'd called a few times and left messages but Owen never called back. He had dropped by the apartment once. He said Owen looked kind of rough but had insisted everything was okay. He had promised to call Liam later that week, but he never had.

Hearing that made my heart sink. Part of me hoped he was just angry at me or busy. Not that I liked either option, but at least when I closed my eyes at night I could imagine he was doing okay. But then Liam said something. He said he didn't know what was going on, but I could try talking to Owen's girlfriend and she might know.

Girlfriend? He said her name was Mary or Marie or something like that. He thought they worked together, but he didn't know much more than that. Owen had only mentioned her in passing. He said that was he hadn't been that concerned about not hearing from Owen.

I called Mr. Patel to see if he'd heard anything. Mr. Patel wasn't there but his nephew said he'd heard Owen had been seeing a girl but she didn't work there. He didn't know what happened but he didn't think they were together anymore. I wanted to know more—it was the first news I'd had about him in weeks. But Mr. Patel's nephew started to sound uncomfortable; I was pushing him, I'm sure. He said he'd tell Owen that I'd called he should call me back. I appreciate that he offered to do that for me, but I know Owen won't call.

No one else seemed to know anything. Not knowing is the worst. I wonder if I should call the police, just to have someone check on him.

Owen

The duct tape and the twine fit nicely on the broom handle. I wouldn't be able to carry them all easily if they were loose. It's a twenty minute walk on a good day when the weather's okay and my body cooperates. Today, neither is the case. It's raining in a steady drizzle and my ankle is aching, my leg is rigid and weak and my ankle brace just feels like it's making everything worse.

Mr. Patel is going to catch me one of these days. Or Vijay will figure out what's going on. I don't care. It doesn't matter. No one cares anyway. She was the only one who thought twice about me.

I don't know if I can save it. I lean against it, resting for a moment. The limb is browning and brittle at the edges and it's been moving slowly towards the trunk. I take the broom and brush away the bits of bark that have started to rot. I'd managed to get most of the smaller broken branches trimmed. But that's not the problem.

The tree has a split at major fork. I've been trying to force it together. I use the duct tape and twine to try and bind the split halves together. It's above my head and I don't have the leverage or strength to do it all at once. Each day I've gotten a little closer.

I used the broom handle and the twine to slowly ratchet the pieces together. The last time I heard the handle make a cracking sound. I don't think I have many more chances with the broom so I hope this does it. I loop the twine around the trunk and work it up to just above the band I made the other day. I loop it off and slip the handle between the trunk the twine and twist.

"You think you're gonna get it today?"

The voice surprises me. I turn to find a middle-age looking man in coveralls and a park department jacket.

"Don't worry, I don't care. You saved me the work in the meantime," he says in between swigs from an oversized Styrofoam cup of coffee. "Not sure why you would do it, though. You one of those 'Save the Planet' types, or something?"

"...No."

"Well doesn't matter to me, either way. But it probably doesn't matter. Doesn't look like you'll be able to save it. Besides, we've gotten some complaints from the residents. If things don't take a turn soon, we're going to have to cut it down."

"...Please."

"Hm?"

"Please don't. I'll take care of it. It just needs some time."

"Hey, if it were up to me, you could have all the time in the world, but I've got a boss, too, ya know?"

I don't know what to say. I feel my eyes burning and my nose starting to flow. My face feels red hot. I'm not going to cry in front of a stranger. I won't.

I can feel him watching me intently.

"Let me give you a hand."

He doesn't let me answer, but just comes to the tree. He adjusts the twine. He's taller than me and can stand upright to get a better angle.

"Let me know if I need to stop," he twists the broom deftly. The broom handle makes the cracking noise again, but he keeps going. It's almost there as the handle snaps in two. He pulls the line up tight and ties it up.

"Well, that does it for your broom, but I think we got it. At least as good as we're going to. Looks solid," he hands me the pieces apologetically.

"Thanks."

"I'll see what I can do. I might be able to buy you a week or two."

"…Thank you."

"It's no bother. Like I said, you've saved me the work. Hope it all pans out for you."

He turns and leaves without another word. He is heading back to a city truck drinking his coffee as if nothing was out of the ordinary.

My windbreaker isn't suited for this weather. Everything is sticking to me; I'm soaked and the drizzle just keeps coming. I start the trek back to the store, but now I have to juggle pieces of broom with the twine and tape.

They can't cut it down. It has to make it. Something has to last.

Micah

Mom has the girls. I had to go by the attorney's office for probate shit. It didn't take nearly as long as they said it was going to and now I have some free time. I have the afternoon off from work. I don't have anywhere to be and nowhere I really want to go.

I pull into a grill pub just off the main strip. I ate here once with some guys from my last job. That must have been seven years ago. I remember the jalapeno poppers were pretty good.

It's early afternoon on a weekday and the place is as dead as you'd expect. There's one waitress wrapping silverware in napkins, a fry cook who's leaning against the bar watching a baseball game and another lone patron in the corner sipping on an iced tea while reading a big book—maybe a textbook, I can't really tell. The waitress is in no hurry as she ambles over to me, although it's not as if I'm in a big hurry either.

"Can I get you something to drink?"

She smiles. She's a little on the heavier side, probably a few years younger than me. Wedding ring. I stopped noticing wedding rings for a while. I didn't really care if another woman was available or not. I was happy with what I had. I was happy with Miriam.

Okay, I went to the strip club with the guys a couple times and I got a lapdance or two. I know she wouldn't like it so I didn't tell her about it. I enjoyed it, but that's not even cheating. That was a moment, nothing more. It was just me gawking like a horny frat boy. I'm a man, that's what we do. But I never did anything inappropriate. I never touched them. We never talked. She ground her ass against me until I got a raging hard-on and then it was over.

And the more I tell myself it wasn't a big deal, the guiltier I feel—maybe that's why she ended up with him. Maybe it was the same with her.

But I saw the texts. She said she loved him. And it wasn't pillow talk stuff. She loved him.

"I'll have Budweiser."

If she'd just fucked him that would have been better. I could have believed it had just happened, that she hadn't meant it. But the look on her face when I confronted her, what she said, what she didn't say—she loved someone else.

She tried to convince me that I misunderstood. She told me they were just joking around. She tried to tell me nothing more had happened, but I'd already seen the other messages—the ones where she was masturbating in our bed talking to him.

She said that's all that happened—just texts and things on the phone. I have no way of knowing. She'd lied before. I had to decide if I was going to put it out of my mind or punish her.

I did want to make her hurt. I wanted to take the girls. I wanted to make sure she never saw them again. She betrayed them. She betrayed them because she betrayed their father.

Maybe that's the problem. I still don't believe her. But I tried. I still try. I try because I love her. Love means believing someone when they're lying to you. You love them because the person is bigger than the lie, even when the lie is horrible.

The beer is gone before I even realized I'd gotten it. I just want to hit something right now. It's moments like these I'm glad I didn't make her tell me who it was, because I think I'd find him and kill him.

But she tried after that. The few months after that were terrible. I didn't know each day if she'd be there when I got home. I didn't know if I wanted to go home most days. But I did. And she tried to convince me each day she'd changed.

I don't know how you prove that. I guess that's the problem. I hadn't been able to tell that she had been with someone else, let alone fallen in love with him. How do you know that things are different when you couldn't tell they had broken in the first place?

I wanted us to be happy. I wanted our family and I wanted us to be together. I wanted to believe her. That idea was worth failing for.

I'm hurt that she wasn't as perfect as I wanted her to be. But she was the one I loved and even imperfectly she was the only one for me.

And that's where it ends. I can't forget her infidelity, but I will not forget what she was to me. I think I understand that now. Miriam will never be an easy thing for me in my memory and heart. She used to be. She used to feel like a natural extension of me. But that's not who she was. And even so, I love her for who she really was, even the parts that hurt.

Someday it will be easier. I'm sure of that. In time those few months won't be as important as our life together. But it's going to take a while.

Miriam, I love you. Goddamn you for not being here.

Thank you.

Mr. Patel

He did it. He broke my broom.

Fuck it. He's done.

He's very strange. I don't need this anymore. I give him a chance and he just acts like a crazy person.

I say this and then Vijay and the wife both suddenly act sad. This is what they beg me for and when they get it, they look at me like I'm an asshole. I can't win. They all want me to do things and then get to nitpick me when I do something. But as soon as they need something then I'm fine again. At least Owen never asked for anything.

Oh well. I've fired hundreds of people over the years. Owen wasn't special. They're all the same in the end.

I call him into the back. I tell him it's time for him to go. I give him five minutes to gather his things and that's that. Sometimes they argue, sometimes they cry—I thought he'd be one of those—and sometimes they don't say anything.

Owen didn't really say anything. He apologized, but didn't argue. He grabbed his jacket and hobbled out the back.

I don't know what will happen to that boy. Not my problem anymore.

Now I have to hire again. Jesus… it never ends.

Myrna

The police officer said Owen didn't want to talk to us. I tried to get more information but he just told me that I should probably leave him alone for a while.

How can they ask me to do that? They don't understand. Something is wrong with him. Someone needs to help.

Burt went by the apartment. He spoke to Owen a little. He had a key and let himself in. Owen told Burt he was fine and then demanded his key back.

Burt hasn't said much since he got back. He tries to assure me I worry too much, but he's worried. I think he's trying to keep me from worrying more, but you don't spend twenty-nine years with someone without being able to tell.

I think we've lost him.

Micah

I had to pick up Sarah from day camp today. She got in a fight with a boy who was a year older and a head taller. Part of me is a little proud that she kicked his ass. Miriam would have winced if she heard me say that.

There's still two weeks until school starts. I was afraid this might happen, but at least it happened now instead of at school. She hasn't said a word since she got in the car.

"What happened today?"

No answer.

"Sarah, we need to talk about this."

"…He was stupid."

"That's not an explanation."

"He was being annoying."

"Really? Is that where we're at? Do you really expect that to count as anything?"

No answer. She's turned almost sideways in her seat, turned towards the window.

On TV I'd be able to say something that she'd respond to and I'd yell at her and she'd cry and then confess how much she misses her mother. She'd be able to say what's been wrong with her—that she thought it was her fault or she didn't say goodbye. But that doesn't happen. She looks annoyed.

Maybe I should make her watch more TV so she knows how this is supposed to work.

She's a good kid. She's going to be okay. I really believe that. She's got a lot of me in her, but some of her mother. Miriam was a force of nature. I never knew anything that could stop her. She was amazing to watch. She'd keep trying and would get frustrated and just when it looked like she was about to throw her hands up she'd stop. Her expression would change. It was like she went to a different place in her mind, like she was able to see the world from a different perspective and it was all as it was supposed to be. Sometimes she'd keep plowing through until it was done. Other times she'd adapt—let the chips fall where they may and get around it. I was always more bullheaded than she was. I'd beat my head against the wall until either the wall won or my head won.

She changed me because as I look at Sarah, I'm not going to beat my head against that wall. It's like I am able to take that step back like she used to. Sarah will be fine. She's determined to beat the world by the sheer force of her will. At some point she'll have to stop. And I'll be here to give her pointers on being stubborn and angry.

Because I am still angry. I've lost so much that was beautiful and just when I was getting it back it was taken from me again. That's not right. It's not fair and if there's a God, I'll never forgive Him.

But I have two beautiful daughters and a family that's supportive of all of us. My life will never be the same. I'll never get back what I've lost. There will never be anyone or anything that will fill the hole that she left. But I have so much that I'm thankful for. Things will be ok.

"They cut it down."

"What?"

She points out her window to a freshly cut stump where the tree that had been damaged during the ice storm in the spring. I couldn't believe they were trying to save it; it was an eyesore.

"I thought it was getting better."

"It was in rough shape. It wasn't going to get better. It was time for it to go. I'm sure they'll plant another one in its place. It'll be just as good in the end. Maybe better. You just have to give it time."

"Whatever. I liked it."

I don't answer as we pull into the driveway. At least she's talking.

*****

Owen (5 months ago)

We were going to go to our usual spot, but the freezing rain interrupted our plans. It was impossible to get almost anywhere. The rain had stopped although now there's a coating of ice on everything. The fog has rolled in giving everything an eerie glow in the street lights.

We came sliding into the parking lot at the park. It's so quiet; no one dares to be out tonight. It feels like we're the last two people on Earth. She's been holding and squeezing my hand as she drove. We've been giggling and giddy—it felt like at any second we were going to slide off the road and kill ourselves. But it's only sort of scary. It mostly feels like an adventure.

The car stops and we don't say anything, we just look at each other. Her eyes are so beautiful, it's like they fill me. I can see everything about her in them.

She tugs my hand playfully. "Let's get in the back," she whispers.

She guides me back. We wrap ourselves in a blanket from the back. We press against each other as we both try to fit under the blanket, or at least that's the excuse we have for wanting to be so close. I wrap my good arm around her and she takes my weak hand in hers. She bites her lower lip with a smile as I lean in to her and we kiss.

"You're so beautiful," I whisper to her.

"Really?" she whispers back, shyly.

"You're the most beautiful person I've ever met."

"You make me beautiful. I'm so much better when you're around."

I can't help my smile. My heart is fluttering in my chest. I kiss her lightly on the neck.

"I have to ask you one thing," I breathe to her.

"What's that?"

"Why are we whispering?"

She giggles with a little snort and then blushes a bright red. I love her laugh. I move my hand down her side to her hip, resting on her leg. She looks into my eyes, there's a moment of concern that flashes across her face.

"Can you just hold me?" she almost apologizes.

"Sure," I smile. She still has a little troubled look in her eyes. I give her a squeeze to assure her.

"We don't have to do anything more. It's enough just being close to you."

She smiles. I can tell when I've said what she wanted to hear. And it's what I really wanted to say. It's like we're two halves of the same person.

She nuzzles into me. She feels so warm, so soft. I never want to let her go. We don't speak for either an eternity or seconds—time doesn't seem to make sense here.

"That's so pretty," she whispers.

"Hm?"

She points out the window. There's a huge old tree covered in ice. The limbs hang low from the weight. Icicles hang off the branches like glass ornaments. The mist has frozen on top giving it a frosted look. There's an unearthly glow from the ambient light and the mist that makes the tree shine dimly like a distant moon.

"It's like it was made for us. It's like this moment—the tree, everything—was supposed to be like this. It's like we're supposed to be right here, right now."

"I want to share everything with you," I say it and then feel self-conscious. There's no way anyone can say something like that and have it mean what they want. No one can be that earnest without it being ridiculous.

She looks at me with that smile, her eyes look right through me. "Me too. I always want you to be close to me."

She lays her head against my chest. I wonder if she can feel how hard my heart is pounding.

I look at the tree. The limbs are so low. "I don't know if the tree can take it."

She glances up at it, but seems unconcerned. "It'll be fine. It's our tree. It's our icicle tree. It'll last forever," she whispers and she wraps her arms around my waist.

I smile. She's right. This moment is ours. It's us. It's beautiful and it's perfect. It can't end. This is my happy ending. This is our happy ending.

I kiss the top of her head and she sighs happily. Someday I'll tell the girls about the icicle tree and this night. Maybe someday I'll get to tell a child of our own about it. I'll get to tell them that sometimes the best things do work out. Every child needs to know that. Knowing that is the greatest thing in the world. She taught me that.

She looks at me and smiles. "I love you, Owen."

"I know, Miriam. I love you too."

9th & Park

I blame the internet.

Urban legends used to have a certain aura. They were mysterious and unsettling. Best of all they were associated with a place you knew—somewhere that couldn't be anywhere else. Now they're everywhere. All the interesting ones have gone the way of the buffalo and in their place have come a myriad of banal stories about uses for Coca Cola, conspiracy theories about big oil, the Illuminati, or the Illuminati controlling big oil while drinking Coca Cola.

But back in the days before the internet, when mass media was still an exclusive tool of three or four major conglomerates, people had their own stories. There were haunted houses. There were mysterious murders and ghost trains, Satanic cults, shadow groups trying to kidnap children, Bloody Mary and unexplained lights in the sky. They were interesting and horrible and fantastic all at once and they were tied to an address—you could go and find the place if you wanted to. What was more, they were often unremarkable places—houses that looked like every other house, roads that were indiscernible from others, common items found in anyone's household. That's what made them so unnerving—it could be anywhere; it could be you.

I'd been collecting and documenting these urban legends, their variations and locales for a year and a half. Ironically, it was for my blog—a collection of stories and accounts of the strange, the supernatural, curiosities and any number of things my mother told me were a waste of time when I was a kid. I suppose I was part of the problem with my little online contributions, but I still think that the homogenization of our legends, fears and wonder is depressing.

I'd be lying if I said that the bulk of people I deal with are nice, normal, regular-type folk. I get a lot of eccentrics, which isn't a complaint—their stories are almost more interesting, if less believable. Then there are the token crazies—my favorite was the guy who wanted me to investigate a one-legged phantom that haunted Wal-Mart. Not just one store, mind you, the entire Wal-Mart chain. I politely declined that offer.

As a result I have a certain natural skepticism when it comes to dealing with people who are interested in my work. With that in mind, I was doubly skeptical when I received a note from an online follower named Thom who promised that he had found the biggest, most mysterious and yet virtually unheard of mystery spot in the country. Hyperbole is a big red flag. And something being so... well, weird, for lack of a better word, is also a big red flag.

The internet is a big place full of all sorts of interesting people who want to make you look like an idiot for their communal amusement. The worst incident that I ever stumbled into was showing up at what I thought was the site of a mysterious 1878 family murder in Connecticut. Instead I found myself walking into a sweet sixteen party for Britni Tomaszewski. I've been careful since not to repeat that kind of mistake.

The e-mailer didn't give many details other than it would be easier to show me than to explain. I sent a generic "Thanks for your interest in my site. I get many tips every year and can't follow up on them all, etc. etc..." and figured I'd heard the last of him. Instead he kept e-mailing and e-mailing, begging and pleading that I come and check it out. He offered to pay for plane tickets, hotel room, and use of a car. He gave his home phone number, references, past employers, and sent a copy of a gas bill showing his address—all unsolicited.

The DMV required less information from me when I got my driver's license so I thought I'd take the chance. I let him cover the hotel room, but I did do the air and vehicle myself. I had to be in the area for an actual work assignment anyway so it dovetailed nicely.

He set up a meeting at a small coffee shop in some obscure nook in the suburbs. It took forever to find even with the GPS in the car. It seemed like a strange meeting point to just go over some photos and whatever else he had, but whatever, it wasn't the strangest first meeting I'd had.

I found a parking spot just around the corner from the coffee shop and walked briskly through the misty drizzle. The weather had been depressing when I arrived and it hadn't given any indication of relenting in the 24 hours since. As I got to the door I received a text. To this day there are few things that seem more unnatural than reading a text from my mother says, "SRSLY WTF!?!?!?! <3 U BB! KTHXBYE!" I didn't even know what she was talking about this time. I think sometimes she did it just because she knew it creeped me out.

I entered the shop. It was a small place—no more than 10 or 15 tables in total. There were only three occupied—one by a couple that looked so happy I wanted to kick a puppy. The second had an older lady absent-mindedly bobbing a tea bag in a cup of hot water as she read an autobiography written by a politician who wanted to run for president. The third and final table was occupied by a nervous looking skinny guy wearing an olive sweat jacket and a black t-shirt. He had an unkempt dollop of sandy hair jutting every which way on his head. I guessed he was probably the one I was looking for.

"Thom?"

He looked startled at first and then grinned nervously. "Are you Dale?"

I nodded and extended my hand. Thom looked uncomfortable but grasped my hand in return. "Good to meet you," I said with a smile I didn't quite mean.

He turned towards the counter, "Did you want something? I'll get it, no problem. Anything you like."

"I'll just have a cup of the house coffee, nothing fancy. I can get it. Please, sit." I had to admit the guy was making me nervous. He squirmed uneasily, eyes shooting back and forth as if he was expecting to get jumped by the plastic plants from the divider next to the table.

"You sure?"

"It's fine," I set down my laptop bag on the chair next to mine and my notepad on the table. "Just keep an eye on my stuff and I'll be back in a second."

He passed the first test by not grabbing my gear and running. Instead he sat fidgety and waiting. As I got my coffee he produced a worn looking notebook from the chair next to him. From what I could tell there were loose papers jutting out the sides and who knows what else. I was starting to think I'd been lured in by one of the crazies. I grabbed a couple napkins and made my way back to the table, still unsure of what to expect.

As I approached it looked as if he was whispering to himself. I realized he was rehearsing. I tried not to smirk as I sat back down.

Thom set the notebook squarely in front of him and took a deep breath. He looked me dead in the eyes and began reciting what he'd been practicing.

"This story goes back almost a hundred years. There seems to have been an older legend before that, but the most recent version started then. They used to call this corner 'Lover's Stop,'" he pointed out the window across the street. "The story went that a couple would come and wait for the bus. At 3 o'clock a bus would appear—but there was never a 3 o'clock bus scheduled. If the couple was there and the bus appeared to them their love was true and they'd be together forever."

It was an odd story. It was definitely fairy tale-ish and a bit more upbeat than my usual fare. I thought that if I was able to get some decent first-hand accounts it would make an interesting entry in my collection. That said, it did sound more contrived than I would've liked.

"Ok, so couple waits for a mystery bus, bus comes, bus leaves, happily ever after—is that the gist of it?"

"Yes."

"…It sounds a little silly."

Thom bit his lower lip anxiously, "Well, don't they all to some degree?"

"Well, I suppose. I guess what I meant is that this one sounds a little too romantic comedy."

"That's what I thought. I mean it's just too neat and clean, right? But the story's been around forever. My mom grew up here and remembered hearing it from her aunt. Ask anyone who's grown up around here and at least half will have heard of it."

I flipped a packet of Equal through my fingers as he talked. The more he talked about how he'd heard about others who knew of the legend the less interested I became. Nothing kills a good legend faster for me than hearing that the bulk of the evidence is being attributed to "them"—the unseen "everybody" who no one had actually ever met but everyone had heard about. I could see the next couple of days talking to a bunch of housewives and cat ladies who had all heard similar things, but didn't have an actual personal experience or even know of someone who had a first-hand account. Basically, no one who would have anything remotely specific or interesting to add.

"So is that all what you've got in the notebook?" I asked, although at that point I'd pretty much given up on any hope that it would be a memorable or compelling story.

Thom's face flushed. "No. I mean, some of it is. But there's more. I-I just can't show it all to you yet."

That piqued my interest a bit, "How do you mean? What more is there?"

"It wouldn't make sense yet. Trust me. Besides, we need to meet Mrs. DiCenzo."

"Mrs. Who?"

He looked at me confused. "Mrs. DiCenzo, the woman who saw the bus back in the 60's. I just mentioned her."

I hadn't been paying attention apparently, but I nodded as if I'd remembered before he'd even finished his reply.

He gathered his notebook and backpack and stood to leave. "It's not far. We can walk from here."

We didn't say much on the walk. The drizzle made it cold; the grey haze made it dreary and my sinuses made it miserable. We walked a couple of blocks and turned the corner and found ourselves in what felt like a different era. The streets were lined by aging townhouses, many in poor repair, but they all looked like they were taken from an old Polaroid picture.

"It's this one," Thom pointed at the lone townhouse with meticulously tended flowerboxes at the window ledge and lining the front steps. I followed him up the step where he knocked and waited for a moment before calling, "Mrs. DiCenzo?"

He knocked again and looked at me sheepishly, "She's hard of hearing, but she said she'd be here today... Mrs. DiCenzo!"

There was a shuffling behind the door followed by the sound of a deadbolt being turned and a security chain being undone. A mop of white, curly hair popped out along with the scent of ancient menthol cigarettes and cat piss.

"Oh, Tommy, I was just in the kitchen and I heard the door."

"It's ok, Mrs. DiCenzo. This is Dale, the man I told you about."

She grinned at me as if I were someone important, "Of course, of course. Won't you please come in? It's a mess in here; I didn't have time to straighten up. Careful so the cats don't get out."

I was pleasantly surprised to only see two cats; one jet-black sitting irritably on the couch and a smaller tabby that was far too interested in harassing a housefly to notice the door was open. I was expecting about 30 just based on past experience.

"You boys just sit down, I'll bring some treats and we can talk in a minute," she said cheerily as she disappeared down a hallway. Thom sat in a wooden chair in the corner leaving a stiff looking chartreuse loveseat. I assumed the recliner with the extra pillow and multiple Afghans was probably earmarked for our host. It totally was the "old lady chair" complete with a TV tray butted up against it that had a TV remote, a box of tissues and an old TV Guide lying on top of it. I sat on the loveseat and surprisingly it was even less comfortable than it looked. I would have thought it would have required spikes or electrical current for that to even be possible.

There was a clanking of glasses as the old woman returned; uneasily balancing a tray with store-bought cookies arranged on a plate and three glasses of… something. She set the tray on the coffee table and then rearranged the cookies so they were in a neat circle again. Thom dutifully picked up a glass and a couple of cookies. Mrs. DiCenzo took her glass and made a neat little stack of three cookies on her TV tray. I didn't really want any of it, but took my glass and a token cookie.

I sipped the beverage and realized it was Tang. I didn't even know they still made the stuff. It tasted much better when I was a kid and thought it would make me an astronaut. Now it was gritty and kind of tepid and horrible in the same way that Saturday morning cartoons were tepid and horrible when you rewatch them as an adult.

"Mrs. DiCenzo, I told Dale about the bus stop. He was really interested in hearing your story if you'd like to talk about it."

She laughed a strange clucking laugh. "Oh come now, you boys don't want to hear some wild tales from an old lady."

Thom gave her a little chiding look and she winked back at him mischievously. "Well, I suppose since your friend came all the way here I could tell him the story." She leaned back in her recliner and eyed me in that way that people who know how to tell a story do, partly casual with an air of indifference but always studying their listener out of the corner of their eye.

"I'd heard the stories for as long as I can remember. You and your beau go to the corner of Park and 9th at 3 o'clock. If you're one of the lucky ones a bus will come and it will stop. The bus driver says something to you and leaves. And after that, the two of you will be together forever.

"Now it wasn't always a bus, mind you. My best friend Lena said her great aunt saw it when it was a horse car. Of course you never know about stories like that. Some people talk just to sound like they know more than you," she chuckle-clucked again. "But it does go to show that the stories have been around for ages. That's all I meant to say.

"Before I tell you about my Anthony, God rest, I need to tell you about Salvador. Now I was maybe all of 15 or 16 and he was 19 and I was head over heels in love with him. You know how girls fall in love? I was all of that and more. I had each of the eight children we were going to have named and their futures planned. I drug poor Sal to that corner every day for a month—a month! And what did I get for my trouble? Walking pneumonia from sitting there three rainy fall days in a row with Sal, that's what.

"I suppose I was being demanding, but Sal was enlisting— this was a year before they started the draft—and I wanted us to be together. I thought that if the bus came it would make everything perfect. We'd have our perfect life. We'd have our eight perfect children in our beautiful house and all the things that my 15 year old imagination could think of that would make life perfect.

"I was stuck in the house for two weeks. Sal left. He promised to write, but you know how that goes. First you get a letter every day. Then every couple of days. Then maybe once a week and then you hear from that busybody Mrs. Fulp that he's engaged to some floozy from North Carolina.

"I was devastated. I was so very melodramatic about it all, too. I'm surprised my mother didn't slap me silly for how I was acting. I mean you look back and you realize how silly it all was, but I guess that's part of growing up.

"So I was heartbroken. I stayed at home and wrote bad poetry; I listened to all the records me and Sal used to listen to. I had an old sweater of his that I kept so I could smell it to remember him. I did it all.

"I stopped going out with my friends anymore. They always wanted to fix me up with some boy and I told them I didn't want any part of it—I was in love with Salvador and someday he would come back to me. After a while I think they got tired of trying to get me to go out and so they just left me be.

"Now, one day I'm heading home by myself, still just moping about. I'd gotten a pebble in my shoe and by the time I decided to do something about it, I had this huge, ugly blister on my foot. So I was hobbling down the street and it was just awful. I was tired. My foot hurt. It was hot and muggy. It was just all-around miserable. I finally had to stop and rest. I sat down on a bench almost on the verge of tears to see what was wrong.

"You know how things like that go—it doesn't really hurt so bad until you see it. Well, as soon as I did that, it hurt real bad," she said with a wink.

"So I don't know how I'm going to get home and my foot is throbbing and I'm trying not to cry and then out of the blue I hear this voice next to me say, 'You okay there, miss?'

"I look over and there's this boy about my age sitting there. He was okay looking, I suppose. My heart didn't skip a beat or anything. He was just unremarkable, I guess. I told him I was fine.

"I was trying to figure out how much further I had to try to get before maybe someone from the neighborhood would see me and give me a hand. I wasn't sure who would be around.

"'Is there anything I can help you with?' the boy asks me.

"I wasn't in the mood for some nosy stranger, but I was trying not to be rude. I asked him what time it was—at least then I'd have an idea who might be home. He pulled out this beaten old pocket watch and told me it was a little before three. Now at that time of day there wouldn't be that many people out and about that could help me. I was just getting angrier and more frustrated with each second and just when I'm about to cry I'm so upset I get a tap on my shoulder.

"'Why don't you take the bus?' he asks me. And I'm mad and my foot hurts so I snap at him, 'There's no bus coming for an hour!'

"Now he didn't get angry or hurt or anything, which was remarkable by itself, I think. He just smiled and pointed down the street. I looked up and there it was. I hadn't even realized I was at 9th Street yet. The bus pulled up and I couldn't believe it. I figured he had the wrong time or I was confused because... well because it just couldn't happen like that, you know?

"The bus pulls up and the door opens and... and I still don't know what happened. The bus driver said something. The boy smiled and nodded and looked at me. I looked at the bus driver and he tipped his cap and told us to 'Be safe walking home,' and then the doors closed and the bus lurched away. My head was in a fog, but the boy took my hand. He looked me right in the eyes and said, 'My name's Anthony DiCenzo. I think I live a couple blocks over from you. Let me help get you home.'

"From that day on we barely spent a moment apart until he passed away in '09.

"That's how I know the bus stop is real. It happened to me when it shouldn't have. It was fate. It brought me and Anthony together and you know what? We had an even more beautiful, perfect life than anything I ever imagined before or after. You see? Sometimes you have to believe in a little magic in the world to make it all worth it."

Mrs. DiCenzo smiled as she leaned back in her recliner again, nibbling on a cookie. She peered at me from the corner of her eye with smug satisfaction, knowing that she'd got me hook, line and sinker with her yarn.

After a moment, I broke the silence. "That's quite a story."

"I've learned if we're lucky, we live stories," she replied.

*****

We headed back towards the coffee shop. "What did you think?" Thom asked hopefully.

"It was a good story. One of the better ones I've heard lately, honestly."

"So you believe her?"

"What?"

"You know, you believe her about the bus stop, right?"

I stopped dead in my tracks and looked at him.

"Are you serious?"

Thom looked at me puzzled and a little hurt.

"Listen, I'm not the 'X-Files' or anything. I just collect stories. They're not true. They're modern folk legends. I'm not some supernatural investigator; I'm more of an archivist."

His head dropped and he didn't say anything for a moment.

"I'm sorry, Thom. I thought it was clear from my website."

We stood there in the drizzle for a minute.

"Well, thanks for all the information and setting up the thing with Mrs. DiCenzo. I'll shoot you an e-mail when it goes up on the site. It really is one of the best stories I've heard," and I turned to leave. It felt like the most merciful thing I could do.

I got a few steps away when he said, "There's more."

"I think I've got enough. It's good."

"No, there's more to the story. I haven't told you about the pictures."

"What pictures?"

"Let's go back to the coffee shop and I'll show you," he held up his notebook as if there were proof inside.

I wasn't sure what I should do. Part of me was intrigued at the idea that there was something more there. The other part of me felt like Thom might be desperate enough that I believe him that he'd overplay his hand and I'd end up listening to a bunch of half-assed 4th hand accounts of vampires working at the local Circle K or something.

"Please Dale, you need to see this. It's the reason I called you here. If you're not interested I promise I'll let you go and I won't say another word, but you've only heard half the story."

"…I don't know. I was going to catch up on some other work back at the hotel."

"Thirty minutes. Just give me a half hour," he pleaded.

I already felt a little bad for lying to him about having work to do. It was a white lie, but I'm a guilty sort by nature. Giving him an extra half hour felt like a happy medium between being a nice guy and not getting dragged into a mess.

The tea lady was still at the coffee shop, other than that there were a few more people but it still wasn't exactly busy. Our previous table was still open and didn't look like it had even been cleared off yet. We both sat again, I glanced at my watch, hoping that time wouldn't drag on too long.

Thom leaned forward and spoke in a hushed tone, as if he were about to divulge state secrets or something.

"Mrs. DiCenzo told you the legend everyone has heard. But you weren't the first person to come investigate it. Before you or I was Benjamin Waller. Benjamin was a grad student doing his thesis on local folklore in 1978. He came in and did the same thing as you, but then he wanted to do some interviews with some locals.

"He first asked around and there were some local kids who said they knew of the myth and went and waited for the bus, but nothing ever came. He realized that he got a lot of interest just because he had a tape recorder with him—I mean those things still weren't that accessible. The people who went around with recorders and microphones were usually newspaper or radio guys back when that was still kind of a big deal. Benjamin wasn't sure if his volunteers were doing it because they believed the story or because they just wanted a chance to be on the radio or whatever.

"What he decided to do instead was get an apartment kitty-corner to the bus stop and he watched it. When a couple came he'd take their picture and then he went down to talk to them to see if they were there for the legend. There were a few that said they were and he got their stories on tape."

I sighed, "I have enough with Mrs. DiCenzo's story. If you've got copies of his work I'll take a look at them—"

"No, that's not it at all. Here," he flipped open the notebook and there was page after page with Polaroid photos stapled to them and note hand-scribbled by them. "This is what he learned—he *saw* the bus, but when he got there only the guy was sitting there," he pointed at man with a letterman's jacket on sitting next to a blonde girl. "The girl was gone. He asked the guy about the girl and he didn't know what he was talking about—he said he'd come there by himself.

"Benjamin showed him the picture and the guy said he'd never seen her before. Now he thought it could have just been a coincidence; that they had arrived at the same time and didn't know each other. You know, she just got on the bus and there was nothing weird going on.

"But he kept taking pictures and it happened again, and again, and again." With each "again" Thom flipped a page and pointed at another photograph.

"He took it a step further and started showing the pictures to other people and no one knew who the other person was in every case. It was like that person didn't even exist.

"Benjamin was getting suspicious that something else was going on, but he never had any real proof. Finally he saw an actual couple—they were all over each other," he flipped to another page with multiple pictures stapled to it with two people kissing and cuddling and whatever else. "The bus came, he disappeared and she said she never saw the guy before. He showed her the pictures and she just got confused and angry and stormed off.

"Benjamin thought he finally had enough evidence that something untowards was going on so he went to the police."

"And what did they do?"

"…Well, they threatened to arrest him for peeping on couples. They thought he was a pervert."

"Was he?"

"Was he… a pervert? No! Well, he was different, but I don't think he got off on it or anything."

"Where is he now?"

Thom looked at the table, "He died eight months ago."

"How did you come by all this?"

"He gave it to me."

"He just gave it to you? Where did you know him from?"

"I knew him from work."

"From work?"

"Yeah, he was at the place I worked."

I looked at Thom for a second. "That's kind of an odd way of saying it. 'He was at'? Where did you work?"

"Look, it doesn't matter—"

"Then tell me where you worked."

"…It was a group home."

"What?!?"

"He had some issues, but he wasn't crazy he was just… sick. He was lucid. He knew what was going on."

"So your source was some sort of mental patient?"

"It wasn't like that. He was there for something else. Listen, I shouldn't even be talking about it—confidentiality and all that. It doesn't matter anyway."

"It seems kind of relevant to me."

"It doesn't matter because I continued his work. I kept collecting evidence," he flipped open to the back page of the notebook where there was a folder haphazardly stuck wedged inside. "It's creepy, man. Seriously, for each story like Mrs. DiCenzo, I have five where one of them just disappears."

He looked at me, and apparently didn't like what he saw. "Here, take it," he pushed the notebook and folder towards me. "It's all there: dates, times, photographs, video. I've spent two years working on this and this is everything I have to show for it. Take it. Look it over. If you think there's something to it, let me know and we can work on it together. If you don't, you might as well just burn it all,"

"Thom, don't be so melodramatic—"

"I'm serious. If I'm the only one who believes in this then it doesn't matter if I have evidence or not. I know what I know. I don't need any of it."

He just got up and left. "Thom, c'mon. Don't be like that. Come and get your stuff." But he just kept walking.

I wasn't about to chase him but I wasn't sure what I should do. Part of me just wanted to leave the notebook and its contents right there and go back to my hotel and not give it a second thought. But I also felt a little bad. I wasn't really interested in taking things any further, but even if it was a complete hoax, the notebook did represent a lot of time and effort. It seemed wrong to just leave it to be tossed out by a disinterested bus boy.

"Just another half hour… I'm such an idiot," I muttered to myself.

*****

I sat in my hotel room half watching Sportscenter, half scowling at the notebook. The notebook had become my Eraserhead baby—I was intrigued, protective, horrified and resented the hell out of it. After spending the GNP of Grenada on my in-room minibar I was finally able to start flipping through the information with only a trace of bitterness.

I skimmed Waller's notes. They started out rather clinical —collections of dates and times, some names if they were available. As time went on, the entries became more descriptive. He tried many times to describe the bus, but each time it devolved into strange descriptions of random items—the amount of sunlight, what the air smelled like, what song was playing on a radio down the street. It was odd.

As time wore on it was clear that Benjamin was having problems. The notes became more and more disorganized. There were several pages where he tried to draw the bus. Most didn't look like buses. One of the last ones looked like a flaming duck.

I moved on to the folder of material Thom had compiled. There were more notes and pictures, but fortunately Thom was at least aware of the digital age. It appeared most of his work was on CD's and DVD's. Since I was sufficiently wasted at that point, it was better I sit back and watch things than try to read anyway.

I slid the first DVD into my laptop. It opened and a list of folders all named for dates came up. I chose one at random and opened it. There were three movie files in it. I opened the first one and got comfortable.

The screen was blurry and then snapped into focus, back out slightly and then locked in as the camera and fixed on its target.

"Ok, here they are," came Thom's voice in a raspy whisper from behind the camera. A couple—a tall white guy and medium height girl with shoulder length black hair—were the subjects.

"Out for a walk? Hmm. Such a beautiful day, isn't it? Look how pretty she is. Tell her how nice her hair looks," Thom narrated. It was fucking creepy.

He was trying to zoom in as closely as he could to them but it was clear he was a ways away, probably across the street in the same cramped studio apartment that Benjamin had used. The result was the couple was large in relation to the screen, but blotchy and pixilated. The couple were holding hands and being snuggly in that obnoxious "only been dating a month" sort of way. They sat on the bench, arms around each other whispering and giggling together—or at least that's how it looked.

"Alright, it's 2:53 on the 27th of April. Haven't seen these two before. Hold on," the camera jolted and there was a loud clunk sound as the video camera was set down. In the background I could hear Thom mutter, "I need to get damn tripod," as there was the sound of shuffling and a zipper.

"I'm going to get some stills of these two," he announced loudly for the benefit of the camera. Part of his back cut into the foreground as he positioned himself. There was a beep and the pointless fake sound of a camera shutter digital camera designers insisted on using on their products. Thom shifted and took another picture, and another and another.

One of my college profs once told me that there was a thin line between passion for something and obsession. He said true passion was about understanding and enjoying; obsession was about possessing and controlling. Thom's position on that continuum was surging towards all-out batshit crazy.

"Ah, shit," Thom said. The camera jostled again and pointed to the street where the couple was heading down the street. Thom sighed loudly, "2:57, looks like they're leaving. Have to try again tomorrow. Goddammit."

The camera pointed towards a table that it had been sitting on but I hadn't been able to see before. It seemed like he was getting ready to turn it off when everything stopped for a moment. Suddenly the camera flew back up and it seemed like Thom was frantically fidgeting with something. The screen went all white and then the camera must have adjusted to the light and shapes started appearing from the glare. There were two figures running. Thom was still juggling the camera so it didn't really get focused on anything but the quick flashes made it look as if a guy and a girl were running towards the bus stop.

"2:58—wait 2:59," Thom was nearly shouting with excitement. "Hold on," he said to no one as he set the camera down. He seemed to try and angle it towards the bus stop but all it ended up capturing was a light pole and part of a tree. I could hear the camera clicking away. "Oh my god…" he whispered.

The camera jiggled and was fumbled and jolted every which way before being pointed at the bus stop. There was a hint of a bus pulling away and the guy sitting alone on the bench. The camera zoomed in on him. He was expressionless, almost bored looking. He looked around for a moment and then stood to leave.

"3:01, there's been contact! Contact!" he squeaked shrilly. "Gotta get down there," and the file was over.

I glanced back through the materials; there weren't entries for each day. I realized he'd been there every day waiting for people to show up and the files left were the ones that actually had something on them.

I opened the next file. "3:08," came a breathless Thom. He appeared to be running. "Excuse me! Hey, excuse me!" he yelled.

When the camera stopped shaking so much it centered on what appeared to be the guy from the earlier video. He'd stopped and was turning towards the camera.

"Hey man," puffed Thom. "Can I talk to you for a minute?" The guy looked confused and a little wary. "C'mon, it'll just take a minute. It's for a research project I'm doing."

He looked at the camera skeptically, but stopped walking. "Ok, but I've only got a minute," he replied.

"Cool, cool. That's awesome, thank you," Thom was still a bit out of breath. "My name is Thom and I just need to ask some general background questions first, alright?"

The man nodded stiffly in reply.

"Cool. First off, what's your name?"

"Adrian."

"Good to meet you, Adrian. Like I said, I'm Thom. How old are you?"

"24."

"Are you in school or working?"

"Uh, both, I guess. Going to school and working full time."

"But primarily a student, right? You're not working a career type job, are you?"

"No, more of a student, I guess."

"Married, single, divorced?"

"Single."

"Single as in not married, or single as in not seeing anyone at all?"

"Single. Just me; no girlfriend or anything."

"Ok, I have a few more specific questions that I need to ask. They might sound a little strange, but just bear with me, alright?"

Adrian looked distrustfully at the camera. "I suppose."

"Have you suffered a head injury recently, have any kind of brain damage or used any kind of drugs or medication, legal or otherwise?"

There was a pause and Adrian started to scowl.

"I swear I'm not a cop. This is all part of a psychology project I'm doing, honest. No one will see it other than me. It's just something I've got to ask as part of the process."

"…No."

"No history of blackouts or seizures?"

"No," a bit more forcefully and getting clearly irritated.

"Can you tell me what you've done in the last 30 minutes?"

"…Listen, I really got to go," Adrian started to turn away.

"Wait! Ok, let me ask you something more specific. Can you take a look at something for me?"

Adrian paused and the camera shuddered again as Thom caught up with him. Thom's digital camera came into frame. He scrolled through a couple photos and then lifted it to Adrian.

"Do you know this girl's name?"

Adrian glanced at it, and shook his head.

"Have you ever seen her before, even in passing?"

Adrian took a second more studious look. "Nope. Doesn't look familiar at all."

"What are your impressions of her?"

"What?"

"Like word association. What are the first thoughts that come to mind when you see her picture."

Adrian squinted at the small camera screen for a moment and then shrugged. "I dunno. She's sorta cute, I guess."

"Anything else? Does she make you feel anything?"

"What? No. Why would she?"

Thom's voice was trembling with excitement. The camera was beeping as he sorted through other photos.

"Do you remember this?"

Adrian looked at the display again. "What? Is that from a few minutes ago?"

"Yes. You were heading to the bus stop."

Adrian looked alarmed when he saw the photograph.

"And you've never seen that girl before?"

"No, I already told you."

"Ok, can you look at this picture and tell me who you see?"

"That's me and…"

"Do you recognize the other person?"

"It looks like that girl."

"Do you remember seeing her?"

"No. She must have just been passing by or something."
More beeps coming from the digital camera as Thom
scrolled through more shots.

"Do you recognize any of this?"

The expression on Adrian's face changed almost
immediately.

"What are you doing? What's this about?"

"Is that you with your arm around her?"

"No. It was just me there. I don't know what you think
you're doing, but it's not funny."

"This is no joke, Adrian—"

"Fuck you, you creepy little prick. How long have you
been following me? Is this how you try and pick up guys
or something—take their pictures like some sort of stalker
and then try to fuck with them?"

"No, I haven't done any—"

"Stay away from me. You take your little freak camera and
keep it the hell away from me." Adrian turned and started
to storm away.

"Please, I just need to know about her."

Adrian crossed the street, seemingly intent on putting
distance between the two of them. The last image before

the file ended was Adrian flipping a middle finger over his shoulder towards the camera from across the street as he marched down the sidewalk.

I sorted through the other folders; they were more of the same. Some of them thought it was a big joke. Some got angry. He made a couple cry. A few just ignored him. They were all compelling in some way. Most seemed as if they could have arrived at the same time with a stranger they really didn't know. Most of the videos showed two people arriving about the same time, one getting on the bus and the other not seeming to notice.

I wasn't sure what to make of it. Well, that's not true; I did know what to make of it. It was the Holy Grail of urban legends—part romance, part horror story. I was just pissed that it had to come from that goofy bastard Thom. I don't usually root against people, but there was just something about him—the neediness, the persistent insistence on something so unbelievable, the whole ass-backwards approach he used. It was maddening.

I'm not sure what time I fell asleep or how many files I'd watched. It was probably less than I thought given the number of empty bottles and the cardiac-inducing incidentals charge to my room that I discovered the next day. I know I felt like hell and that apparently I'd slept through two phone calls and about a dozen texts, most of them from my mom. ("CLL ME L8R, LOL XOXO <3 MOM") I was surprised that none of the calls or texts were from Thom.

It was nearly 12:30 by the time I finally decided that the discomfort and boredom of lying in bed was greater than the misery of being ambulatory. I started up the hotel coffee maker and took a shower. The shower did make me feel marginally better and the coffee at least gave the back of my mouth a better taste than the pickled death that I'd woken up with.

I flipped through some e-mails and on-line comments to the site, but I really wasn't giving them my full attention. I knew I probably should go back to the bus stop, preferably around three just do my own follow-up.

The debate in my head raged on: I didn't report, I recounted. It didn't matter if the phantom bus really existed at all. My work was about people and the stories they tell. On the other hand, I'd spent nights in "haunted" houses before and spent nights in secluded clearings waiting for mystery lights in the sky to appear. I never saw anything, of course, but I'd still done it.

I rationalized that actually going to the sites helped the narrative. I was able to turn the experience into a first-person account—it helped me to describe the place: its smell, the aura of it. But what was I supposed to do if I went to the bus stop, describe the smell of piss where the homeless guy had relieved himself the night before? And when did going to a bus stop become sort of moral crisis? The whole thing was taking on a life of its own and my role seemed to be growing exponentially when all I'd wanted to do was write up a snippet and move on.

I had a day before I had to get to my real job. I'd originally hoped to do a little sightseeing or at least some cavorting, but that seemed less and less likely as I slowly conceded that I really didn't have much of a choice. Once I'd made up my mind my irritation and resentment largely dissipated. Funny how resentment lies more in the deciding than the doing, isn't it? Any resentment I felt after the fact came from blaming the choice I'd made on someone or something else.

I was doing the latter as I stood outside. The previous day's drizzle had evolved into a full-scale rain overnight. I was trying to shelter myself underneath an awning by a trendy little bistro. From the looks of the staff that came by the window they didn't seem to appreciate my presence next to their establishment. I hadn't packed anything too heavy and nothing remotely water resistant so once the moisture had worked its way into to the jacket I was wearing it felt like the cold had worked its way into my bones.

I stood shivering under the awning staring at the bus stop. I get cranky when I'm cold anyway and the cold and rain gave me the opportunity to examine many of my life choices. I determined that I was, in fact, a fucking idiot. I was freezing my ass off, hung over, staring at a bus stop that I didn't expect anything to happen at. My cousin Dirk had gotten a degree in business administration. I made fun of him: his lame degree, his ill-fitting suit and his uninspiring nine to five office gig. But then again, he wasn't getting dirty looks from a testy assistant manager wearing ironic retro glasses and enough hair product to make the mess on his head almost look unintentional at 2:48 in the afternoon in some eddy of a town.

My mom had texted me again. She used "STFU!" although I don't think she knew what it actually meant. There was a jingle behind me.

"Sir, you can't stand there."

I turned to find the pissy-looking hip-glasses wearing douche guy poking his head out the front door doing his best to convey his displeasure. I looked at my watch: 3:02. "Yeah, whatever," I answered as blew into my hands and mentally prepared to walk through the rain back to my rental car.

I had planned on going and getting something to eat then heading out for the evening, but after a rather joyless serving fajitas and a watery pilsner I opted to go back to my hotel and wrap myself in the comforter until I wasn't shivering anymore.

As I sat, engulfed in sheets and blankets, the TV in the room next to me blaring something in Spanish, I really began to wonder what I had been doing with my life. I didn't want to be Dirk, but I was pretty sure I didn't care enough about what I was doing to be feeling this miserable. I had to get up early the next morning in order to catch a meeting for my actual paying job in a suburb on the opposite side of the paved serpentine highways, bypasses, exits and tollways of the city. I hated that job and its cubicle and inane acronyms, but at least there might be something like it somewhere else that didn't suck.

My job had become an ex-girlfriend—still driving me nuts, but in my weaker moments I remembered just enough potentially good things to make me wonder if something could've worked. My phone vibrated as a text came in.

"HEY BB WRU? CALL ME! XOXO M<3M"

It was so wrong.

*****

Morning came abruptly. I felt much better but still drained. I parted the blinds in my room and for the first time since I'd arrived actual sunlight broke through. It was almost blinding at first but it had the same effect on me that it had even back in grade school—I didn't want to go to work. I admit I'm kind of a big baby with that, but it was especially rough after a stretch of crap weather. A nice day has the power to instill a deep-seeded and primal urge to play hooky.

I don't think I'd really decided to skip out of work right off, but looking back I certainly mulled about and dawdled when I knew I didn't have the time. I consciously avoided looking at the clock, doing what little I could do to put off any guilt or chiding from the voice of responsibility in the back of my mind. You can't be held accountable for being late if you had no idea what time it was—at least that's what the 10 year old in my brain insisted.

When I finally did look my stomach sank. I wasn't going to be just a little late. It was bad. My inner 10 year old was quick to assure me that the sinking feeling in my stomach was indication that I was sick and shouldn't go out. I needed to call in sick. The grown-up part of my brain really didn't want to call in sick, but given how late I was going to be, it would at least be an easier story to sell than I was just horribly irresponsible.

When I was a kid doing the "sick voice" was easy—sound as nauseous, hoarse and miserable as possible. As I got older though I realized that the "sick voice" was a lot like the "hung-over voice" which often would do more harm than good if you used it. I suspect most adults have encountered a similar conundrum at some point in their lives.

The solution I found was to sound miserable, but to also sound optimistic. So instead of calling in and saying, "Ohhhhhhhh, I'm so sick," I'd say, "I'm sorry I'm not there yet, I've been feeling kind of rough this morning. I'm trying to get my stuff together. I think the throwing up is mostly over so I should be able to make it in in an hour or so." The latter often gets you an order to stay away if you do it right, thereby getting you out of work and, as a bonus, relieving your conscience of responsibility for the decision. My inner 10 year old was distressingly crafty at times.

I made the call and then went back to bed in an obligatory attempt to at least act sick for a while. I dozed lightly but was soon too restless to even lie quietly. I turned on the TV and browsed through 40-odd channels of bland late-morning talk shows, game shows, re-runs and up-to-the-minute news soundbites. I felt antsier by the minute and it seemed to double each time I flipped to a new channel.

Some of it was guilt because I knew I wasn't really sick. But there was more. My mind kept going back to Thom and the bus stop.

There aren't many stories that hold up to scrutiny. I don't just mean in the true or false sense: most stories become just another series of events when they're dissected. If a street magician is able to do some astounding mind-bending bit of sleight of hand part of you wants to know how it's done, but for me the bigger part is just happy to be astounded. Achieving that sense of wonder is harder to get as I've gotten older. That's partly why I did the website. I didn't want answers; I wanted to believe there was something unknowable out there.

But I'd gotten close enough to Thom's story to where if I learned it was all true it would be the most amazing, horrible thing I'd ever experienced. As it was, the story was good enough, but the temptation to go further was irresistible.

I started to think of it in solely hypothetical terms to begin with: if I were to go back, I'd wait just down the block. Or if a couple were to show up I'd try and stay close to hear what they're saying to see if they mention anything about the legend, etc. Soon that turned into actual planning and once an actual plan was formulated it really was just a formality that I was going to do it. I knew that it was a one in a million chance that someone would pick that day to go to the bus stop but like a gambling addict, I had to give it just one more shot.

The plan was solid. Thom and Benjamin had always focused on the person left behind. But what about the bus or the rider? If you could figure out what happened to them then you'd have an answer, too. I sat in the rental car watching a block down from the bus stop. In my zeal I'd gotten there way too early and was stuck sitting, waiting, running the plan over in my head again and again and again.

It felt like forever. I looked at my cell phone for the time and it was only 2:26. I watched people walk down the street and wait at the bus stop, studying them for any clue that would give them away as a believer. A bus came and picked up a few people around 2:40. I used it as an opportunity to time things out in my head—how long it took them to board, how long it took the bus to pull away, how long it would take me to catch up with the bus from a block away, and so on.

I was going crazy waiting so I tried to clear my head. I flipped through the radio, settling on a sports talk show. I played Tetris on my phone, always stealing glances at the bus stop to see if anything had changed. My mom texted me a picture that her friend Gloria had sent her of a cat in a flowerpot. "OMG SOOOOOOO CUTE!!!!!!!!!!!" I used to think that the string of obnoxious forwarded e-mails was the most annoying thing she could do. The text messages were worse by far.

My extra grande latte a few hours prior had taken the express lane and now was in my bladder demanding to be let out. I waited as long as I could in hopes that it would just go away, but I just couldn't hold it any longer. I slipped out of the car and jogged across the street to the coffee shop. The lady behind the register gave me a dirty look as I hurried by to the men's room. After relieving myself I came back out and waved apologetically to her hoping that she at least remembered that I'd given them my business a couple days before.

I rushed back to the car. Time had become an abstract concept. I knew it had probably been at most five minutes since I left the car, but my mind was racing and I was worried that I'd missed it, or not given myself enough time to prepare. It was worse than trying to get to sleep the night before Christmas when I was a little kid.

2:49.

I went through the plan in my head again. Arranged everything in the car to where I needed it to be. Started the car so it was idling and ready to go.

2:50.

I was slowly driving myself insane. I focused hard on the radio. They were talking about on-base percentage. I didn't really care about it, but I made sure I absorbed every possible scrap of information. Then there was a commercial break.

2:56.

It was finally getting close enough to the time where staring at the bus stop wasn't just a complete waste. There were more people out and about; the break in the weather certainly seemed to have helped. There were people coming and going which kept me a lot more occupied than the day prior when I just had to stare and wait.

A guy and a girl—looked to be in their early twenties—turned the corner together. She seemed to be chatting away, laughing and gesturing. He seemed to be intently listening with a studious expression. They looked like they could be possible targets.

They kept walking down the street together. They got to the bus stop and stopped. My heart was in my throat. I looked at the time: 2:59. A dull roar came up from behind me and a monolithic wall of dirty white rumbled by with the smell of diesel following closely behind. The bus pulled up alongside the bus stop just as some dude in a hoodie decided to run in front of my car. When he passed the bus stop only had the guy sitting there. The bus pulled away and I swooped in.

I pulled up to the bus stop and lowered the passenger side window and leaned over.

"Hey!" I yelled at the guy on the bench.

He looked it me puzzled and pointed at himself as if to say, "Who, me?"

"Yeah. Who was that girl?"

"What girl?"

"The one you were sitting with. You were talking together"

He shrugged looking completely confused. I didn't even say goodbye but hit the gas and sped down the street. I turned down the street I thought I'd seen the bus disappear down. It was already a block ahead of me. I sped down the street hoping some poor bastard wouldn't decide to jaywalk at that moment because that would surely be the end of him.

Just when I thought I was going to catch the bus I caught a light. I almost ran it but a police cruiser crossed the intersection. I felt frustration, excitement, panic and rage all that same time as I waited the eternity for the light to turn green. The bus had gotten stopped as well a couple blocks down, but it was turning again. I took off again, but realized that there was no way I'd make the light the bus had been stopped at so I turned a block early.

The side street was much clearer and I flew down a couple blocks, doing quick glances down the avenues for a chance to catch a glimpse of the bus. I saw nothing so turned a couple blocks down and re-connected with the last street I'd seen the bus on. I turned on it but still couldn't see anything. I was scanning both sides of the street frantically looking for some sign that it had been there. It was gone. Vanished.

I was about to find the nearest bar or drive the car off a bridge (I hadn't decided which yet) when in the translucent reflection of a store front down the street I saw what looked like a bus pulling away. I braked hard and the tires squealed as I stopped dead in the middle of the intersection. I turned hard and hit the gas, lurching forward wildly towards the bus. It was a great white whale of metal and glass and I was Captain Fucking Ahab.

I sped down the street and turned the corner and I saw her —the girl from the bus stop. She was alive. She wasn't in some alternate dimension. She hadn't been swallowed by the Earth; she was just walking down the sidewalk.

I turned in and parked as close as I could and got out and ran after her. I caught up to her and touched her shoulder to get her to stop for a moment. She turned towards me. "Can you hold on for a minute, I've got something over here," she said. It was then I saw the Bluetooth earpiece she was wearing.

"I'm sorry, I thought you were someone else."

She waved me on, "Ok, I'm back. It was nothing. So next week should be fine…"

And I had my answer. Or at least a plausible answer. She hadn't been talking to him; she'd been chattering away on her phone and it had all been a coincidence.

My shoulders sank as the sense of disappointment and anti-climax set in. I felt stupid for getting so worked up over something so improbable. Suddenly all the excitement and intrigue that had built up during the process of learning about the bus stop and the legend was gone. It was more than gone; it had turned into something obligatory and joyless

I headed back to the car. In the meantime mom had texted me again, "FWD: FWD: FWD: FWD: FWD: FWD: PLEASE keep this goin. Hi, my name is Erick Bruce. I'm 7 yrs old, I have a larrge tumor on my brain & severe lung cancer. The doctors say I will die soon if this isnt fixed & my family cant pay the bills. 'The Make A Wish Foundation' has agreed to donate 7 cents 4 everytime this message is sent on. Please help me."

I wished I'd never gotten her a cell phone for her birthday two years before.

*****

I sat at the table feeling surprisingly nervous. I felt like I had to make sure Thom got his stuff back, but really wasn't looking forward to the meeting. I hadn't even called him, I'd just texted him saying I was going to return his documents and to meet me at the coffee shop the next day at 10.

I nursed my cup of coffee although I was completely disinterested in actually drinking it. The cup gave me something to fidget with at least.

Thom came in looking disheveled and sullen. I waved and did a half-stand in greeting as he came to the table.

"Here's your folder. Thanks for letting me look over it."

"Did you even read it?" Thom snapped.

"…Yeah, I went through most of it."

Thom scowled at the table. "You going to use any of it?"

"Yeah, there was some good stuff in there."

That seemed to agree with him. He looked up and only looked guarded instead of angry. "So you saw the video clips?"

"Yeah, I checked out a few of them."

"So you saw it. It's just like I told you, right?"

"They were certainly compelling," I answered, hoping it didn't sound as non-committal as it actually was.

"Okay, so now what do we do?"

"Well, I have to get the article together—"

"Yeah, but what's our next step? I mean, I know you might have to go back, but I can keep investigating. I can get more information and follow up with the people I see. Maybe we can get more people to help when the story gets out—"

"Uh, Thom, I think you have the wrong idea."

"What do you mean?"

"I'm just doing the article."

"I know, but you saw—"

"Things aren't always how they look, Thom. Listen, it's a great story, and I'll my best to do it justice but—"

"But it's not just a story. I've seen it. I've talked to them —"

"Thom, I followed the bus yesterday. No mystery, it's just a normal bus."

"But people are being erased from reality!"

"No, Thom. They're just strangers at the bus stop. I saw the whole thing."

"Well, what you saw must have been a fluke. I've seen it a hundred times."

"Thom, do you really think that the most logical explanation that I witnessed yesterday was the fluke? I'm sorry, but I just don't believe that."

"But you just said you saw it—"

"I did, but when I investigated it further it ended up being exactly what you'd think it would be. It's a great story Thom, but it's just an urban legend."

"No, no, no, no," Thom was on the verge of tears. "You don't understand. It's not."

"Why is this such a big deal to you?" I meant to just think that, but instead realized I'd said it out loud.

Thom reached into his back pocket and pulled out a worn, folded piece of notebook paper and slammed it on the table.

"I didn't meet Benjamin by accident. I mean he was at the home I was working at, but he found me," Thom started unfolding the page. It appeared to be a page from Benjamin's notebook.

"He asked me if I remembered the 9th of June, 2006. I didn't know what he meant and then he showed me this," Thom flipped the page around. It was a journal entry from Benjamin's notebook.

"June 9th

2:57 a couple approached the point, and sits. Seem to know each other.

2:59 bus comes into view

3:00 bus leaves, male left at point, female gone.

Unable to reach male before left observed point"

"I asked him what that had to do with me and then he showed me this," Thom produced a worn photograph. From the angle, it appeared to have been taken from the loft across the street. It was a younger, clean-cut Thom sitting back on the bus stop, smiling. There a pretty blonde girl next to him, smiling as well. They weren't looking at each other, but if I'd seen the picture in any other context I would have thought they could be together.

"See? I don't know her. I don't remember ever seeing her before in my life, but there she is. She was sitting right there and then she was gone."

"Thom… if you don't remember her couldn't it be because you never knew her?"

"I had to of," he turned the photo back towards himself. He ran his fingertip around the outline of the girl's face. "I had to have known her. I looked so happy. We were happy together..." his voice trailed off.

Thom smiled sadly and murmured to himself, "I was happy with her once…"

*****

I never saw or heard from Thom again. I returned home and wrote my story. I got in a medium amount of trouble for skipping my meeting. The bland reproach of my supervisor was a welcome bit of punishment in contrast the vision of Thom I had—alone, desperately clinging to a memory of a love that never was.

It haunted me for months in a way that nothing had before or since. I hoped that somewhere he found some peace and was doing perfectly horrible, boring things like the rest of us. But deep down I thought he was probably still at his loft every day at 3pm, snapping pictures, making videos and waiting for the life he wished were true to be returned to him on a phantom bus. In the meantime he'd hover there, unseen, writing logs of the comings and goings of the strangers below—always looking for the final piece of a puzzle that just wasn't missing one.

Labor Day

"Is that you?"

The screen door slapped the doorjamb carelessly as the sound of claws on linoleum and the jingle of a collar came from the kitchen. Pisces' nose appeared jutting out from the kitchen wall.

"We're back. You get some sleep?"

"A little," I lied. Pisces came into the living room and nudged me with her nose. I waved her off as I broke into another fit of coughing. Pisces lay down at my feet, looking up. She'd seen this enough times to know I wouldn't be able to give her any attention until I could breathe again, but she was willing to wait patiently.

I can't even remember when breathing was easy.

Tara leaned against the doorway. I must have looked bad because she got that pity look—her eyes widened a bit, her forehead wrinkled and the corners of her lips hinted at a frown. It was like she was looking at a sick pet.

"Do you want some lunch?"

When she didn't know what to do she offered food. Some days I thought it was really endearing. On the bad days it just annoyed me.

"I'm not hungry."

"Something to drink? There's still some of that pomegranate juice left. You said that helped a little last time."

"I'm fine. Don't worry about it."

Pisces had stood and was resting her head on my leg. I scratched her ears and she closed her eyes and panted happily. She seemed to know what I needed more than any person. Then again, my expectations for her were a lot lower.

"I don't have to go tonight. I can call Jan and tell her I can't come. She'll understand."

"It's ok. Go. I'll be fine."

She looked at me like she wanted to say something. Or wanted me to say something. Or just wanted it to not be quiet anymore.

"I'm going to call them."

"Jesus Christ, I'll be fine."

She didn't say anything. She just watched me quietly wheezing on the couch with that look on her face. That look spoke volumes—I knew she cared, but I wasn't even an adult to her right now. I was a sickly, wheezing infant that needed to be coddled and kept. When trying to ease my discomfort wasn't enough and there was nothing she could do but watch me tremble and cough, then she'd just feel bad for me. I didn't want her pity. Seeing that look just reinforced what I already knew—that I was pitiful and dying. The thing I missed the most was how she used to look at me like I was her support—her shoulder to lean on —not some burden.

She was biting her lower lip. That's what she did when she was upset but wasn't sure what to do.

Now, I've gone and hurt her feelings. Fuck.

I knew I was going to feel bad for snapping at her later. But that would be later. For now I just wanted to be left in peace.

It was one of my bad days and nothing was going to help me through it. But that didn't mean I felt like being treated like an object of pity for the rest of the day.

I could tell she wasn't going to go to Jan's. As soon as I went to the bathroom she'd call them and explain that I was too sick to be left on my own. Maybe she would just duck out of the house for a second using Pisces as an excuse and call from outside. That was the lie we lived. I'd pretend I didn't know what she was doing. She'd pretend that she hadn't wanted to do it anyway. She probably wouldn't even say anything; she'd just wait to see if I'd notice. Deep down it seemed like she wanted me to be helpless so she could do something. At least when I was dependant on her she could figure out what to do. Part of me hated her for that.

"Your mom called earlier," she said, still studying me from the doorway

"When?"

"You were in the bathroom."

"What did she want?"

"She just called to say hi. Wanted to know how you were doing today."

"What did you tell her?"

"I said that it was a rough day."

"And?"

She sighed and cocked her head. She was about to tell me something she didn't think I wanted to hear. "I told her that you won't go to see the doctor."

"Goddammit Tara, why'd you have to do that?"

"She asked if you'd gone in. I'm not going to lie to your mother. I've lied enough to her."

"Fuck, not this again."

She was standing, arms crossed, almost like she was cold. "No, I didn't mean it like—" she stammered and trailed off. She looked at the ground and murmured, "I just don't like lying to her," to the floorboards.

She always managed to bring up the baby thing like it was some kind of fucking trump card.

I was sick and Tara was still in school at the time. I think she chose to forget the facts and just imagined that everything would have been fine if it weren't for me. We even had "the talk" and both agreed we weren't ready to have kids. Never trust a woman who agrees with you too easily, I guess.

She'd never so much as disagreed with me. She cried a little but she said it was because it was all so sudden. I'll admit I didn't want to get married and a kid is a popular excuse to do it. I must have been deluded because I should have known Tara wanted more. I couldn't understand how our situation could have possibly fulfilled any of her dreams of family life—married, miserable, husband unable to breathe, a dog, a kid all in a little two bedroom shithole. Just what every girl dreams of.

When she took care of it I saw it like she was acknowledging that I'd been right. No one but us and the folks at the clinic knew so there were no distraught mothers, aunts, sisters—it could just fade away like it never happened. We didn't have to worry about any of that bullshit. When I'd asked her about it she told me she was fine, that it was all for the best and it just hadn't been the right time. God I'm a sucker.

I started coughing again. My chest burned and my stomach ached. I tried to sit up straight and look better than I was feeling. I curled upwards, my chest rumbling with a limp hiss of a wheeze following it. I probably wasn't doing a very convincing job at appearing as anything other than a formless, asthmatic-sounding mass of flesh lumped on the couch.

Tara looked at me with a look that said, "Put your balls in my purse and just let me enjoy your helplessness. I'm tired your attitude." We'd done this dance enough times.

She knew that I wasn't going to budge and that I wasn't going to talk about it anymore just as I knew she'd go into the kitchen or the bedroom and call her sister. She would speak in whispers for an hour before explaining how I was a bad partner but she couldn't leave me. Then they would reply how she was better than all this and I didn't deserve her. She'd agree and talk half-heartedly about leaving me more to appease them than because she intended to. I was the thing that made her a martyr after all—you can't just walk away from martyrdom. Then she'd intentionally ignore me for a half hour or so.

Pisces sighed and flopped down at my feet.

Tara turned back into the kitchen. I heard the phone beeping as she punched in her sister's number followed by inaudible murmurs.

I leaned back in the couch as far as I could so I was staring at the ceiling. I tried to connect the dots in the texturing. I found a pretty lifelike profile of Bob Crane in the specks.

I felt sticky. It felt as if the air had settled like the sludge at the bottom of an aquarium. I thought about opening a window to get some air moving—an act of desperation given how my body would react to whatever allergens were floating around outside. Still, a bit of relief might be worth an hour or two of extra misery.

I parted the blinds just a crack. It was bright and the warmth radiated off the window and the opposite side of the blinds. It must have been hot outside—too hot to make it worth opening anything. I let the blinds slip closed again. Looking outside made me sick to my stomach.

Pisces jumped up on the couch. She burrowed underneath me bumping me off to the side and taking up one whole cushion. My clothes stuck to me. I'm sure I smelled horrible. Sometimes the warm water from a shower helped, but I didn't think it would do much today. Pisces had claimed her corner of the couch so I wouldn't be able to lie back down. The bedroom was too hot to sleep in and

Tara would be in and out of there anyway. By process of elimination I was deciding that a shower would suck the least.

"Are you going to be long?"

I pretended like I didn't hear her and closed the bathroom door.

As the steam rose, my breath began to come easier. Even the warm water made me feel a bit cooler and fresher. It wasn't a magic cure-all but it did help me feel better.

It's funny how when you can breathe how your mind gets clearer. I realized I probably should apologize to Tara. She meant well. We'd done this enough times and she knew that I didn't mean anything when I snapped at her. It says something when her biggest fault was not leaving me. As the water ran down my body I started thinking over things again.

The week before she had tried cajoling me into going to some new Mediterranean place downtown. I don't know why she always tried to get me to go out when I was so sick I could barely move.

I should let her go grab some take-out from there and then we could have a nice little dinner here. That would be nice. Plus it could be a little way of making amends for being an ass earlier. It would be nice to do something for her.

The water was turning cool. I didn't know how long I'd been in showering—it must have been a while. Pisces was whimpering and scratching at the door.

"Tara, Pisces needs to go out."

"Tara?"

"Goddammit."

I opened the door and Pisces scrambled in, circled my feet and bolted halfway to the door. She stopped. Sat for a moment looking at me, then ran to me, and then back halfway to the door and sat again.

The cooler air hit my lungs and they instantly seized up. I was hacking and coughing all over again, although it hurt a little less after the shower. I threw on a pair of shorts and an old t-shirt. Tara must have just run out for a minute I thought. I opened the back door and Pisces darted by in brown blur.

The car was gone. It must have been around 5:30 since the neighborhood SUV's and 4 door sedans were returning to their roosts. Pisces started barking at the neighbor as he got out of his car.

"Pisces, knock it off."

Pisces came bounding back in a couple minutes later smelling of dandelions and dog shit. The first place she always ran when she still stank was the couch. I didn't even try to stop her.

Tara had grabbed the mail at some point and left it stacked neatly on the table. I flipped through them: insurance bill, auto shop ad, a clothing catalog and a medical bill for Tara. I opened the medical bill. I hadn't remembered she'd been sick lately. The bill didn't say much. It was a reminder for a follow-up appointment and some lab work.

I read it carefully, trying to get some clue about what it could be about. You can never be too careful. If she was hiding something then it would be good to know about it sooner rather than later. At least then I could use that information if I had to. She was always big on honesty and being open with each other, but people like that are always the first to try and bury something. I tucked the bill back in the envelope and replaced the mail so it looked undisturbed. She had to be back soon.

I nudged Pisces over and fell into the couch. My chest was starting to hint at an ache again. It was going to be another long night. I flipped through the channels and there was nothing on. I settled on a movie I'd seen years ago. It wasn't any better than I remembered, but the actress had nice tits and at some point coming up she'd be running around in a wet t-shirt.

The phone rang a few times but I didn't want to talk to anyone. My mom was the only one to leave a message and it was for Tara. No one wanted to talk to me—not as if there was much to say to me, anyway.

Everyone felt bad for Tara. She was giving up so much by caring for her sick boyfriend, they said.

Truth was if she hadn't met me she would be an assistant manager somewhere by now instead of being an assistant manager somewhere else. They act like she was going to be the president or something. But she's exactly where she would have been anyway, except she'd probably have to pay her own rent.

No one cares about me, and I'm the one who was slowly drowning in mucus-y shit.

The light was starting to dim in the house. Everything was eerily quiet.

Where the fuck is Tara, anyway?

She didn't go to that thing at Jan's did she? Now she's popped off without saying anything. Figures. I'm hungry. I'm barely able to stand and now I'm supposed to try and what—cook? She could have at least left a sandwich or something to heat up if she was going to be gone for a while. All that after I try and do something nice with the take-out thing. Just watch, come tomorrow she'll be complaining how we never do anything or how she wants to go out but doesn't want to leave me alone. It's always the same.

Another fit of coughing had me doubled over on the couch. I was coughing so hard I started gagging, producing little more than the sticky mucus that wouldn't go away. My eyes were watering and my forehead was drenched in sweat as I tried to catch my breath.

Fucking Tara.

I was hunched over on the couch, my chest rattling with each breath. My throat burned.

I just wish I had some pomegranate juice.

Always Get the Check

A wise man once said you should never meet your heroes. I think more broadly you should never meet anyone you really want to be impressed by. He wasn't my hero by any stretch of the imagination. But he did have a certain reputation and a level of street cred that dwarfed just about anyone or anything else you could think of.

I really did it on a lark. It wasn't even a lark; it was more an expression. I said, "I'd sell my soul to get some of that." ("That" was the house, money, car, fame and slew of incredibly attractive groupie types that Corey Burton from "Jimmy Hoffa's Missing Head"—new album in stores now!—had at his disposal.)

It's not like I'm religious or anything. Who hasn't said stuff like that before, seriously?

A week later I got home from work, grabbed the mail on my way in and tossed it on the table on my way to the fridge to grab a beer. After popping open a nice cold Rolling Rock, I began sorting through the letters. There was an office supply catalog, an advertisement sent to "Occupant", a gas bill and a couple of credit card solicitations. As I was grouping together the ones I was going to throw away, one of them caught my eye. I had almost missed it because it looked like a credit card mailer —no return address, "CONFIDENTIAL" stamped in the corner—you know the type. I was about to toss it when I flipped it over and on the back was a little hand-written scrawl that said, "Corey Burton? You could do better..."

I re-read it three times. It was just such a random thing to write on an envelope. It was funny that someone would add such a bizarre comment to a piece of bulk mail so I felt they'd at least had earned the courtesy of me opening their letter.

The letter itself was unremarkable aside from the fact it appeared to have been typed—like with an old typewriter "typed"—and was written out in a format that I hadn't seen since junior high. Mrs. Barajas made us do every example in the formal letter-writing chapter in our English textbook.

666 Acheron Drive
Suite B
Sheol, SC 29874

August 24th, 2009

Mr. Barnard "Arnie" Wells
6122 Pacific St
Omaha, NE 68106

Dear Mr. Wells,

Thank you for your offer. Although we were impressed with all your soul has to offer we feel that we must pass at this time. We receive so many offers that we cannot possibly come to agreeable terms with all of them. While we do see a lot of potential with your soul, unfortunately it just wasn't up to our standards.

We hope you can find a suitable venue for your soul and wish you all the best in your future endeavours. Please keep us in mind should you have any other deals you think would be a good fit for us.

Sincerely,

Abaddon B. Marduk
ABM:tgf

At first I laughed out loud. Someone had to be messing with me. Then I got to thinking—I'd been alone when I'd mumbled my "wish"—at home, doors and windows closed. I hadn't said anything to anyone else about it because it wasn't something I'd spent that much time thinking about.

It was definitely weird. I puzzled over the details off and on for days. How could anyone know that? Who could have known that *and* been clever enough to actually write something like the letter? Clearly the idea was to make me think that it was some sort of demonic, "Robert Johnson at the crossroads" sort of thing. Of course if I had a hard time believing in God, the idea of the Devil was nearly laughable. Still, the whole thing did feel a bit, well, spooky.

My curiosity slowly became indignation: I mean, c'mon, you couldn't tell me Corey Burton—that emo playing douche with more hair product than talent—had a better soul than me? It wasn't even funny. I mean, it wasn't as if I wrote crappy songs and wore pants that were two sizes too small while trying to look all pouty in music videos. Seriously, what the hell?

It gnawed at me over the next couple of days. There were plenty of houses, money and sparkly things to go around. I wouldn't have needed the Devil or whoever Abe Marduk was to get those things. All I really needed was a personal favor from Bill Gates or Warren Buffet. Or even a successful drug dealer. No supernatural hocus pocus, no sinister deals, just a check from someone whose concept of pocket change would be enough to keep me up to my neck in vapid pleasures for years.

I knew it was all some sort of prank. But by the third day I was tired of not knowing what their aim was and, worse yet, feeling like I was dancing at the end of someone else's line like a marionette. I looked up Abbadon Marduk and, surprisingly, he was in the phone directory. Who's in the directory anymore?

Finding him there actually made me feel a bit better— at least I could start to see what angle they were trying to work. Whoever it was just found some poor patsy in the phone book and put his name on it. Of course the real joke would play out if I called the guy and got a bewildered reply or a strip joint or Church of Scientology or something. But it really wouldn't work if I called expecting it to be a prank. I could turn it around and let them know I was onto them. *That* would be the way to get them back—show them how lame it was.

I was rationalizing everything so I could justify taking the bait without admitting I was doing exactly what the prankster wanted. I was hooked and even if I ended up looking like an idiot my curiosity was overriding any other considerations. I had no idea who could've done it, why they did it or how intricate the plot was and the only way to find out was to jump in headfirst.

When I first called the number I almost hung up right away. I hadn't felt that giddily stupid since I asked out Heather Krupal in 8th grade. The phone rang once, then twice. I was about to hang up and pretend like nothing had happened when there was a click and I heard: "Mr. Marduk's office."

The voice on the other end sounded like whiskey gargled with a pack of menthols and filtered through the lady at the Post Office who sounded like she was talking through her nose.

"...uh I got a letter the other day—"

"Was it an offer or a decline, sir?"

They actually sent stuff out? I had to admit; whoever was behind the prank was absolutely killing it.

"Well, I'm not sure it actually came from you. I think it was a prank."

"Can I get your name, hon?"

"What? Why?"

"I can look it up by your name and I can tell you if we sent you anything or not."

"Oh... Uh, Barnard Wells."

"Hold please—" and suddenly I was listening to a marimba version of "Girl From Ipanema".

It was ridiculous. Whoever had cooked this up was both incredibly devious and desperately needed to get laid, I thought.

"Mr. Wells?"

"Yes?"

"Yes, thanks for holding. I'm looking a decline letter that we sent out last week. Looks like Mr. Marduk decided to pass on your offer."

"Ok, wait. What exactly do you guys do?"

"Mr. Marduk offers a wide variety of goods and service in exchange for specific commodities," the lady recited disinterestedly as if she'd said it a million times before.

"Who are you guys, really?"

"I don't know what you—" the woman was interrupted. There was a male voice in the background interjecting something. "Hold on please, sir."

She didn't put me on hold this time, but she was covering the receiver so it sounded like a television across the hall at a cheap hotel. I only heard her side of the conversation: "Barnard Wells... uh huh... No you sent a decline last week... Oh, I have no idea about any of that, that's— I've got it right here... Okay—"

"This is Abe Marduk," came the male voice suddenly on the line.

"Uh, yeah, I was just speaking with someone."

"Taffy told me you were calling about a decline letter you received."

Taffy? It had to be joke. "Yeah, I think there was some sort of mistake."

The man chuckled, "It's ok, Arnie. Can I call you Arnie?"

How did he know I went by Arnie? Barney was more likely given my name. Or he could've called me Barnard. That would have been more appropriate since he didn't actually know me.

"Uh, sure."

"I don't usually take calls on the declines, but I remembered yours specifically. Listen, I'm going to be in Omaha next Thursday, would you like to grab lunch?"

"Um, I'm not sure. I might have something going on."

"That's fine. Like I said, I don't usually talk to people about declines, but I had a proposal of my own that I wanted to run by you."

I involuntarily blurted out a laugh. "You want to make a counter-offer?"

He chuckled good-naturedly. "No, no. If you have a new offer I can take a look at it, but no. I had something else in mind. Listen, I've got to run. I'll pick you up next Thursday at, say, one o'clock. Sound good?"

"I'm not sure. Like I said, I think I might have something
—"

"Alright, great. I'll swing by and if you're free we can grab something. My treat. Listen, I got a thing I've got to get to right now, but we'll talk real soon." The line clicked and that was it.

I had a few days to reflect on that conversation and the more I thought of it the weirder it seemed. Not weird in a compelling way, but in a creepy "I'm not sure what the fuck is going on, but I don't want any part of it" sort of way.

When Thursday rolled around I decided I was going to be just about anywhere but home at one o'clock. I was probably trying too hard since I went to an Office Max at the other end of town to buy a stapler I didn't need. On my way back to my car with my superfluous stapler in tow I stopped to grab an ice latte from a Starbucks. For some reason walking around with a cup of Starbucks always made me feel a little more inconspicuous—a special type of suburban camouflage. I was about halfway across the parking lot when an old light blue Plymouth Reliant pulled up alongside me.

I couldn't see the driver's face, but I could see him lying across the front seat trying to roll the passenger side window down as he was keeping pace to me. I stopped and leaned over to peer into the car. The driver was a balding, paunchy white guy who looked to be in his 60's. He was wearing a white polo shirt with blue and beige horizontal stripes across the top. I hadn't seen that style of shirt outside of TV re-runs from the early 80's. The old man smiled and waved when he saw that I'd stopped.

"Hey, glad I caught you. I was trying to get your attention, but I still haven't got the damn horn on this thing fixed yet," he seemed to realize that he was sprawled across the front seat and sat up and straightened his shirt in order to look a little less awkward. "Here, I'll pull in up here," he pointed at a parking space up ahead, "then we can talk like normal people."

The car coughed uneasily as he hit the accelerator and swung into the parking space. I didn't recognize him. He was probably a friend of my dad's or something, I thought. My dad seemed to know everyone.

He got out of the car huffing and puffing as if flopping around before and getting himself together now was a chore. As bad as the shirt looked, it got worse. He wore navy blue pants, gray and white Velcro jogging shoes and a fanny pack. It was a look that had never really been in style but still appeared among the senior set… 25 years ago.

On his belt he had what appeared to be a beeper. I didn't know they even had beeper service anymore. To top it off he had a digital watch, but not the type with the plastic/rubber wrist strap. It was one of those watches with the shiny metal band to make it look more, well, classy was what they were going for, I suppose. The only thing missing was a cabbie hat.

"Aw wait, I forgot my hat," the man turned and paused for a second. "You know what? I'll be fine. Bald is beautiful, right?"

"Um."

"So Arnie, I could kill for a good Rueben. I know a place."

I was simultaneously incredulous, skeeved-out and intrigued. It had to be a joke. The thought that this guy was supposed to be the Devil was ludicrous. It was more unsettling to think that this old man had been digging up all sorts of personal information on me. He did seem harmless enough physically, though, so I decided it couldn't hurt to at least see how much crazy I was dealing with.

Now when I think of the Prince of Darkness I usually think of either something dark and menacing or extreme opulence that's still sort of menacing. Where I found myself was in a little diner called "Norton's" that I'd passed a hundred times before. It was an aging, cheap-looking place. The tables were well-worn Formica and the booths were (once) shiny vinyl—the type that makes farting noises whenever you move. The place smelled of grease and gravy. It wasn't bad, but it was definitely in the "greasy spoon" camp.

"Go ahead, order whatever you like. I'm buying," he urged.

I wasn't that hungry, but he seemed insistent. "The Rueben is excellent, just a suggestion," he grinned.

The waitress came to the table. "Can I get you guys something to drink?"

"I'll have an iced tea—now is that sweetened or unsweetened?"

"It's sweetened with lemon flavor," she gestured back to the soda dispenser. "It's not brewed here or anything; it's just the stuff the Coke guy has." Abe looked disappointed for a moment, then he smiled.

"That's fine, I guess. I'll get whatever he's having, too," he gestured towards me.

"Um, I'll just have water."

She scribbled on her little notepad. "I got one iced tea and one water. You know what you want to order yet or do you need a moment?"

"I think we're just about ready, love," Abe answered. "What kind of soup do you have today?"

The waitress looked over her shoulder back towards the kitchen and craned her neck as if she could see what was left. "We got a beef and barley, chicken noodle and… vegetable." With the last one she craned her neck and stood on her tiptoes as if she was magically able to see into the large vats.

"You make those daily, right?"

"Every morning, sweetie," the waitress grinned.

"Ok, I'm going to have the Rueben, extra sauerkraut, French fries instead of chips and a cup of that beef and barley soup."

There was a pause as the waitress caught up with him. She was mouthing the words as she wrote. She finished and looked at me expectantly.

"I'll have the turkey club."

"Did you want fries with that or just the chips?"

"Just the chips are fine."

"Okay…" she was mouthing turkey club. "Anything else?"

"You gotta have one of their soups. They're really tasty," Abe advised.

"I'm not all that hungry—"

"Nonsense, he'll have a cup of chicken noodle." He looked at me for approval. "Chicken noodle? You like chicken noodle, right? Yeah, chicken noodle."

The waitress looked at me and I nodded weakly.

"Alright, I'll get you boys your drinks and your food should be up in a few minutes," she scooped up the menus and disappeared into the back.

Abe leaned back in the booth and studied me for a second with a smirk. "So… you don't think I'm the Devil?"

And there it was. The elephant in the room had been given a name.

"I definitely believe you want me to *think* you're the Devil," I countered.

He chuckled. "I suppose you're right. I mean the Devil is supposed to be riding on a horse of fire that eats puppies, not in a K car, right? I'm not a very convincing ruler of the underworld, I suppose."

"Well, that's one way to put it."

"Listen, I know how it looks and, believe it or not, I prefer to keep it this way. I'm really just a simple low-key working stiff like you. I just have a pretty notable job title. I try not to let it go to my head and really, aren't the simple pleasures in life the best?" He looked me in the eyes gauging my response for a second before grinning again. "I suppose me saying I want to look this way and surround myself with these things isn't really proof, is it?"

And in answer my initial question—a shitload of crazy, I determined.

"You just thought that I'm a shitload of crazy," he laughed. I felt the blood rush out of my face like I'd just been caught in the middle of telling a dirty joke by my grandma.

"That's just a parlor trick, really. How about something more impressive? The first time you jacked off you were thinking of the Pink Power Ranger—nice choice by the way. You hit your neighbor's cat when you were driving home drunk after a party your junior year in high school. You hid it in the back dumpster. You still feel guilty about that."

"Uh."

"I mean, this is all trivial stuff. There's a lot more that I do, but you guys really only get interested with the flashy stuff," Abe sat up and smiled invitingly as the waitress came back and set the drinks on the table. "Thanks, darlin'," he said softly with the hint of a drawl. He sipped the tea, making a slight face at the first taste. "You know, they used to brew their own here. It really was a nice touch. Anyway, where was I?"

I stared blankly.

"That's right, me being the Devil and all. Well, as you might imagine there are a lot of misconceptions about me, what I do, and all that. But sometimes you have to go with the legend instead of the truth—it definitely makes for more interesting reading," he chuckled again.

My mouth was dry, but I was able to get enough saliva to speak. "So you're trying to say you're not evil?"

"No, no. I try not to think in grandiose terms like that. I mean, I'm not all that nice really, but then again who is?

"I'm painted as the big, bad source of all evil in the universe but honestly, that's complete crap. I was the first —I definitely earned that distinction. Honestly, that is a source of some pride for me, how many people can say they were first at something, right?"

"So you're saying you're bad, but not *that* bad?"

"Something like that. Let me put it this way, who is Alan Bean?"

"Alan who?"

"Exactly. You've heard of Neil Armstrong though."

"Yes. Of course."

"Well, Alan Bean was the fourth man to walk on the moon, but no one knows who he is. In some things you're either first or you're not really much of anything—there's a certain prestige to being the first. I'm the Neil Armstrong of sin. I set the standard. I forged the way. But I'm hardly responsible for everyone who's come since."

"So you're trying to tell me you're just a regular guy?"

"In a manner of speaking. I'm ridiculously old and have a few perks due to my previous station. But at the end of the day I go home, grab a light beer, and listen to the wife complain about how I don't work around the house. Then I'll eventually mow the lawn or something just to appease her even though I don't really think it looks that bad yet. Afterwards I have some dinner, catch a re-run of Matlock and then head on to bed. And the next day I get up and do it all again."

"Wait, you're married?"

"Sure. Going on 40 years now," he reached back and pulled out a wallet and flipped out some pictures. "That's Mary—ironic name for my wife, right? Anyway, we took that at Branson last year. Here's one when we were at Niagara Falls a few years ago. Here's one with the kids—"

"Kids?!?"

He looked at me like I was crazy. "Well yeah, kids. That's what people do. Your parents should have explained that to you a long time ago," he said with a wink.

"Here's Marty, he's doing his internship in pediatrics in Baltimore," he pointed at the picture of a toothy, red-headed young man with an awkward grin.

"That's Jackie. She stays at home with my two grandkids. Her husband works for Dow so they moved to Delaware for his work. The wife wishes they were closer, but you know how it goes. She's actually going out there for a week in a later this month.

"And this is Eliot," the last picture was of a younger looking man with a scraggly beard and baggy unkempt clothing. "I guess every family has one of them," Abe chuckled. "He's a good kid. Smart. But he dropped out of college his junior year and has been hiking across Europe for a couple years now. We were hoping he'd finish school first, but he's his own guy. Always has been. His mother isn't very impressed with what he's doing, but I tell her that he just needs some time to find what he cares about. I didn't settle down right away either, after all."

Abe smiled and flipped the pictures back into his wallet. I didn't say anything. He looked at me with a grandfatherly smile.

"See, I'm just like you. Or just like people you know, I guess. I just have a more interesting job."

There had to be an angle. There was more at work here, there just had to be.

"So are they all the Anti-Christ?"

Abe had been sipping his tea, he lurched forward, spray a bit from his mouth as he burst out laughing. "Does Eliot look like he could be the Anti-Christ? C'mon. I love the boy, but at this point I don't think he could probably manage the night shift at a White Castle.

"No, they're just people. They've got some of my genes, which means they'll probably live to be 120 or something. Eliot will probably go bald," Abe shrugged.

"So what's your plan? What are you doing with them?"

Abe shook his head. "Listen, you're dad's a dentist, does that mean you're plotting for ways to put fluoride in the tap water?"

"Um."

"No. No it doesn't. I mean you might, but it's up to you, isn't it? I'm sure if your father thought you'd be happy as a dentist he'd try and make it happen, but he wouldn't force it.

"Listen, look at it this way—let's just assume the stories are all true: that there's some big end-of-the-world kind of battle where I don't fare so well. It's a very grim outlook unless the Norse or Manicheans were right, then best-case scenario I tie through mutual destruction, which is just sort of depressing. In other words, it's not exactly the kind of outcome you want for your kids, is it? You want your kids to have soccer games, homecoming dances, first kisses—the whole shebang. Leave the end of the world stuff for someone else.

"But we're losing the plot here. I didn't ask you here to defend who I am or what I've done. That's not all that interesting anyway."

"Well, why did—" I didn't finish because the waitress appeared with our food. Neither of us said a word. I realized I still wasn't hungry. Abe on the other hand attacked his sandwich. I took the spoon and swirled the soup watching noodles, chicken and vegetables tumbling over each other and then disappearing inside the depths of the broth.

Abe had inhaled the first half of his sandwich and had paused for a sip of tea and to catch his breath. He glanced up at me with a look that was a little embarrassed. "Sorry about that," he dabbed the corner of his mouth with the napkin. "Like I said, I love the Ruebens here."

He slowed his pace, gingerly folding the napkin and placing it by his plate. He took a couple more spoonfuls of soup and then straightened in the booth.

"So, here's the thing. I didn't ask you to lunch because I wanted to make a deal for your soul. I asked you here because I want to offer you a job."

I choked on my water, and grabbed my own napkin to cough and hack into for a moment. Abe sat back patiently and waited for me finish.

"I've been doing this a lot of years but the last few, well, the wife wants me to slow down a bit—spend some time with her. Maybe buy an RV and drive cross-country, see the grandkids, stuff like that. Well, I've put it off as long as I can. She finally tore into me a couple weeks ago—said I wasn't following through on what I promised, that I wasn't making time and so on and so forth.

"Thing is, she's absolutely right. I've been married to my work and she's been a trooper for years and years. I've always provided for her and the kids. But I realized I'd only been giving her the things she deserved, not the life she deserved. I need to fix that."

I must have looked puzzled because he smiled and shook his head. "You might understand it when you get to be of a certain age. Or maybe not. Maybe you won't make the same mistakes I have. But trust me, it's easy to get used to putting off what you really want to do until after a while what you really want to do is keep putting it off."

"So, wait, you want me to come work for you? Like, starting wars and stuff?"

"No, I just collect souls. I know it's hard to believe given all you've heard growing up, but I don't have that much to do with natural disasters or mass murderers or any of that nonsense. That's a whole different animal and if you're really curious about the how's and why's of that you probably should be asking the other side. I'm just a businessman. I trade in a commodity. Think of it like gold, or cotton or oil."

"Why souls? What can you do with them? And why should I help you?"

"Ahhh, now we get to the interesting questions. Unfortunately I can't explain most of it to you. For the 'why souls?' question, let's just say they have great value to someone who, for my own reasons, I wish to maintain a level of connection with. As for what I can do with them, maybe nothing. But that's like asking what you can do with a brick of gold. You can't go the 7-11 and buy a Slurpee with it, but it's still valuable and, in the right circumstances, you might be able to buy everything you ever wanted with it."

"So people use their souls to buy things from you?"

"Well, yes, but that's not what I was referring to. There's a bigger picture, Arnie. I have my foot in a whole different world and in that world I need capital. Souls don't have any particular value to me just like a gold brick wouldn't mean much to you on a desert island. But you'd hang on to it just in case you manage to make it off someday, right?"

"I suppose so."

"Doesn't hurt at least, right? Anyway, that's about all I can tell you about that. There are rules and such. Suffice to say that they are a premium for me and that's why I do it."

"But why would I help you? Why don't you just ask me to kill a baby while you're at it?"

"See, you people, I just don't get it. Why do you always assume I have interest in babies or the helpless? And why do you assume that I somehow do it for the pleasure of inflicting pain? Do I look like some sort of sadist to you?"

"Well, no, but—"

"But, but, buttered bread—it's lunacy to think I want to see you in pain. I'm like you. When I watch the news and see that a tsunami has taken out half of southeast Asia, I don't wring my hands and cackle. It's horrible to see so much suffering and pain and death. I mean, just from a business standpoint do you know how many souls are just lost to me when things like that happen? Even if you think I'm some sort of angry, merciless monster, there's no pragmatic upside to it for me. I'm not an idiot."

Abe was actually flustered. He took a big swig of tea and sat silently for a moment. I felt unnerved by it and nibbled away at the corner of one of my sandwich halves. Abe exhaled sharply and looked at me and smiled again.

"Sorry, I get a little worked up sometimes. It just gets my goat, you know? Let me start over again. Maybe when you hear what I'd be asking you to do that will answer some of your questions.

"It's actually quite simple. You'll receive the offers, review them and, if you think they're a good investment, close the deal, determine terms and conditions, etc."

"But why would I do that? Are you trying to get my soul for some sort of weird trading powers?"

"No, I'm trying to get you for 150k a year, plus medical, dental, a housing stipend, a pretty good 401(k) plus the chance to make additional bonuses based on performance. Like I said at the very outset, you can keep your soul. I'm offering you a job, not a way of life."

"You want me to sell out the rest of humanity for 150k a year?"

"I guess it depends on how you mean 'sell out humanity.' If you mean profiting while taking advantage of your fellow man, I suppose I am. But here's my perspective on it: if I were Wal-Mart for example I'd be asking you to sell out humanity for a lot less than that. But in that context, selling out seems socially acceptable to most people, although perhaps a bit distasteful.

"But that's not the point. I'm not asking you to do anything shady. I'm not asking you to lie, cheat or steal. You're just a broker. It's even easier than that. We've got a spreadsheet for determining a soul's value so you don't even have to assess anything. It's a cake job, really."

"Well if I'm not suppose to lie, cheat or steal, how am I supposed to get all these souls?"

"That's the beauty of it: they come to you. You don't have to try and sell anyone anything if you don't want. I mean if you want to go above and beyond, then by all means, but I'm not asking you to do that."

"Well aren't you supposed to try and convince them that they should give up their souls for something? I read Faust; I know how it's supposed to work."

"Well, the sensational always sells more paperbacks. The fact of the matter is they almost exclusively come to me. They offer their souls in exchange for the usual suspects—money, youth, power. Those happen to be things I can do, so sometimes a deal can be struck. But I don't try and seduce them. You all are so eager to seduce yourselves. People want to believe there's an easy way to be happy. You'll go to any lengths to acquire stuff—not even interesting stuff, just boring stuff—and you hope against hope that it'll stop being stuff and turn into magical happy-making stuff." Abe made finger quotation marks as he said "magical happy-making stuff" to emphasize his point.

"I mean, it's like no one's ever read a poem—no great thinker or artist ever said 'The best thing in life is no mortgage and a steady income where you're the boss of everyone and no one tells you when to go to bed.' You ever think why that is? It's because deep down you all know that it's just stuff—regular, silly, worthless stuff. But when someone gets their mind set on something you can't really talk them out of it. Look at the DH in baseball— horrible, horrible idea, but couldn't change it now even if you wanted to."

The waitress walked up to the table almost if on queue. "You guys interested in any dessert today?"

I shook my head 'no,' Abe bit his lower lip thoughtfully. "What kind of pie do you have today?"

"We've got apple, cherry, lemon meringue and a slice of pecan left."

"You sure you don't want any?" he asked. I shook my head again. He shrugged and looked to waitress. "I think I hear that piece of pecan calling my name. Oh, and could I get a cup of coffee to go with that?"

"Sure, hon. Regular or decaf?"

"Decaf, please."

She cleared Abe's plate and bowl. "Are you done with yours?" she asked. I'd finished the soup and most of the sandwich. I nodded and slid the plate and bowl towards her. She scooped them up in a fluid motion. "I'll have your pie and coffee out in a sec."

As she left Abe shook his head, "Back in the day I'd be drinking pot after pot of coffee. Nowadays just keeps me from sleeping. Drives the wife nuts. She made me promise no more regular coffee in the afternoon. It's not so bad, though. Decaf has gotten a lot better over the years."

He studied me for a moment. "I can tell you still have some reservations. Listen, it's fine, I understand. But I did bring this," he reached around and unzipped his fanny pack and produced a folded sheet of paper. He slid it across the table to me.

I opened it. It was a release form. A standard-issue, boring old release form. Except instead of a monetary amount listed, it listed Gary Jarmillo's soul. It had been filled out in its entirety except for the signature.

"Everyone has to sign one of those. And I don't accept them the same day. They have to wait at least 24 hours before I'll take it."

"Is this just a copy? There's no signature."

"I know. I thought it was important that you saw it. I've got drawers upon drawers of ones just like this. There's no signature because Gary changed his mind.

"I thought this might help show you what I've been saying: no one is forced to enter into a deal. When Gary didn't sign I shook his hand and wished him all the best. I didn't send an army of little demon beasties to eat his dog or anything. I don't work like that."

I looked over the form. It seemed so trivial, but if this was all real then it was ridiculous that something so monumental was reduced to a paint-by-numbers document template. I wasn't sure what to make of it. Three weeks before I didn't even believe in such a thing as a soul. I was pretty sure I still didn't, but the implications of being wrong seemed a lot more significant than they had.

"Listen, I know you've got a lot to think about, Arnie. I can't convince you that I am who I say I am or that there is such a thing as a soul or any of those big philosophical questions. What I can prove to you is that my checks don't bounce," he produced an envelope from the fanny pack and slid it over the table to me.

"No obligation. This was just to compensate you for your time today and for your discretion. I'm sure I don't need to tell you what the implications of this kind of information are. I'm taking a chance on you Arnie, but just like Gary if you say no, I'll shake your hand and wish you the best and you'll never hear from me again. But you'll have to get your own ride back to your car," Abe said, face locked in stony earnestness. Then he burst out laughing.

"I'm just kidding. I'd still give you a ride back to your car."

I didn't know what to make of him—he was a strange deliberately absurd little man. He reminded me of my first Little League coach. I had to walk to his house to get a ride to practice. His wife would always get the door when I rang and she guided me downstairs to a big rec room. The room was decorated out of 1974—all wood paneling on the walls, weirdly ornate lamps, faux wood carving ornaments on the walls and in the center of the room there was a mammoth console television. It was one of those old TVs that looked like a giant TV screen had been eaten by a chest of drawers.

He'd always be sitting in a leather barcalounger watching a rerun of "Three's Company" drinking scotch out of a monogrammed whiskey glass. He'd greet me with a "Hey, Slugger!" and had me sit down on a big blue/green floral print couch while he finished watching the misadventures of Jack Tripper.

During the commercial breaks he'd make small talk, usually about how I was going to knock the cover off the ball at practice even though I was ridiculously bad at baseball. He'd usually amble back to his mini bar to get freshen up his own drink. He'd always come back with a second whiskey glass with ice and ginger ale in it for me.

As I looked at Abe I had the same feeling. Both of them seemed to be from a different world or time where they were classy men of the world even though it seemed to be a world that they inhabited alone. Both of them seemed happy about who they were as people, but there was a certain... I don't know—melancholy maybe? But then you could never really tell. They both were operating in a completely different realm. I thought they were both likable in a "born to lose" sort of way.

"So, are you saying I won't have to do anything evil to work for you?" I asked.

"It's more complicated than that. I know every asshole says that to cover their asses, but give me a minute to explain.

"Evil is what you make of it. At the end of the day it's really about what you can live with. And I'm not just saying that as the Devil. You can't get through life without doing something to hurt someone, somehow—not anymore. You buy a t-shirt at the Gap—you don't steal it, you don't swap tags, you just outright pay for it like a good upstanding citizen. You think you're in the clear, right? But to get that t-shirt made they have a bunch of 9 year olds in Malaysia or some damn place working 14 hours a day for eight cents a week.

"Does buying that t-shirt in a perfectly legal manner make you evil? Bad things get done with that money—bad things that if you just think about for a minute will be painfully obvious. Heaven forbid you drive an automobile that runs on gasoline. It doesn't take an economist to see that you're funding any number of morally questionable things with that purchase. Does that make you a bad person?

"The answer is that I don't know. I really don't. If you think about it, there are lots of really horrible things going on in this world but there aren't very many really horrible people out there—and I'm talking about horrible people that go out and do incredibly horrible things. There was only one Stalin or Hitler, and they're long gone. But even without purges and concentration camps and all of those horrors people still keep dying every day. So who's responsible? I just don't know.

"I do know that most people are incredibly unhappy and with each step they take only gets them one step further away from what makes them happy. Hell, look at me. I missed my daughter's college graduation because of work. I don't remember my anniversary half the time and it's taken me almost 40 years to follow through on the promise I made my wife before we were married to take time out for her. I know I'm 'the Devil'—" he did the finger quotation marks again when he called himself the Devil "—but really it's those omissions that I feel guilty about. I lose sleep over those things and at my age with the things I've seen, it takes a lot for me to lose sleep over anything. But when it comes to stuff like that, I think most people do the same thing and it's just as bad whether you're the Devil or Joe Schmoe. You follow me?

"So will evil happen because you work for me? Probably. But no more than any other job you'd have. It's up to you to figure out how to have a clear conscience. What I do— what most people do, I think—is I ask myself about the immediate effects. Will me doing X cause Y? I don't worry about what happens because of Y because it's just too big. If the butterfly knew about Chaos theory would it still fly? Of course it would because you've got do what you've got to do. In the end, big consequences aren't the result of the actions of one person. And if you can't blame one person, then you can't blame anybody, really."

A silence fell over us. The waitress had come and gone already with Abe's pie and coffee and now he was pushing the crust around idly with his fork.

"You're a stand-up guy, Arnie," Abe said finally. "That's why I chose you. You'll have access to a ridiculous amount of power, but you're a company man—I think you'll approach it like a job and nothing more. That's the kind of person I'm looking for. Someone in it for any other reason would be more of a liability than anything else. But I think you'd be good at it for the right reasons. I'm a pretty good judge of character like that. Comes with the territory I guess."

He sounded sincere. I still wasn't sure what I wanted to do. Some of it would depend on whether the check cleared, but the more we talked the more I was convinced that it probably would.

"So what if I took the job and then someone made an offer and I didn't want to do it? What if I just couldn't bring myself to do that to them?"

"Listen, like I said before, it's whatever you can live with. If you only want to take the souls of child molesters and people who kick puppies that's fine by me. I mean your bonus check probably won't be huge with the likes of them, but you won't hear me say boo about it. It's completely up to you."

A shrill beeping interrupted us. Abe reached down and brought up the pager to eye level and squinted at the display.

"I didn't know you could still get service for those," I said.

"You can't. I suppose you could say it's a tool of the trade. People would look at me funny if I walked around with a supernatural glowing orb that whispered to me whenever Taffy was calling to remind me of a meeting or the wife wanted me to grab some eggs at the store on my way home. I always did like pagers. Nifty little things. So there you go. Besides, I don't get cell phones; too many bells and whistles. Why would you want to have your phone take pictures? It's unnatural."

Abe tilted his head back as if he were trying to read the pager with bifocals on.

"Oh, looks like Taffy has got me scheduled for another meeting this afternoon. She's efficient, that one. Not much for conversation but a helluva secretary."

Abe gestured to the waitress indicating that he wanted the check.

"I don't mean to cut this short, but I've gotta catch this meeting. I hope I answered most of your questions?"

"Well, most of them I guess."

"Well here's my card. If you have any more questions about the job feel free to give me a call, alright?" he handed me a perfectly banal looking business card with his name, address and phone number. Part of me still thought that it should burn with black fire or something.

"Now I'm going to say two things before we go. The first is about the job:

209

"I don't want an answer today. I don't even really want one tomorrow. You wait until the check clears—that should clear up some of your doubts. But once it does, and if you're interested you let me know. If you want to go ahead and do it we'll set up another meeting where I'll go over the details, have you sign some paperwork, W-4's, ID verification, the usual kind of stuff. Then we'll go over your contract and if it all sounds good we'll get you signed up and set up with your own pager.

"The second thing is a salesman trick I learned a long time ago. I think you're going to take the job, I really do. Part of it is because I think you'd be a good fit, and you know that. The other part is because I am a helluva salesman and the fact you're sitting here today listening to an old man with a story like mine is proof of that, I think.

"Now here's a tip from an old-school salesman: The easiest way to make sure someone knows you're for real, that you're not trying to scam them and that you're a man of your word is this—" Abe turned and handed the waitress a bill. He smiled and waved her off, "Keep the change.

"What you need to know is this: you always get the check. It's making the first move. It's showing them you value their time and that you're a man of your word. Remember that. It'll make you an eight-eyed man in the kingdom of the blind."

*****

That was almost three years ago.

He was right; I took the job. I was a little squeamish about the soul thing at first, but Abe was right, it wasn't like I was forcing anyone to do anything. They came to me and I'd give them the best deal I could. Most of them took it; some of them didn't and I was glad for the ones that didn't. It seems brave of them to give up on their dreams in the name of a principle. You have to admire people like that.

When they find out I'm not the Devil it usually takes a bit of explaining. So, usually over lunch I tell them a bit about him. That's when I tell them they should never meet anyone you want to be impressed by. I tell them about the K car, about the horrible shirts, the fanny pack, the baldness. Most of them seem disappointed at first. I guess we all want things to be so much bigger sometimes. Or maybe it's they want some sort of pomp and circumstance when they come to barter away their soul.

It was like how my first girlfriend described losing her virginity—there was this stigma and fear and a sense that the world would never be the same. And when it was over her only thought was "That was it?" I think deep down we want things to mean something, for better or worse. But it's like Abe says, losing your soul doesn't feel any different if you sign it over to him or if you let it slowly bleed away for 30 years behind a desk. In the end it's all about what you can live with and what you can get out of it in the meantime.

I explain all that to them and they seem to understand— especially after the 24 hour waiting period. Of course the ones who don't sign probably don't think of it that way.

Maybe my perspective is a little skewed because I really only have contact with the ones who are serious about it, but I think most of them are on the same page.

In the end they get what they want, Abe gets what he wants, I collect my paycheck every two weeks and everyone is happy. I get to meet all sorts of interesting people and talk about things that are important to them. We share a laugh or two and a sandwich or some sushi or whatever strikes their fancy. I give them the pros and the cons. I listen to their concerns and answer their questions. And at the end of the day, win or lose, we part as friends.

And I always get the check.

The Stars Shone Like Callie

for AMK

It was my year. Or more to the point it was my mother's year but she was laid out with a flare-up of shingles. Aunt Dorsey was in Linz on her quest to find more extended family members to talk shit about and Seth, well, it wasn't his year so we weren't sure where he was.

It had rained in the morning, but as the day wore on it became light grey and hazy. As the afternoon slowly bled into evening it felt like it wanted to get warm outside but instead settled for cool and stuffy in a way that made everything feel feverish and clammy. The gravel on the road popped and rumbled as I navigated the country road. As I drove the fields that flanked me started being interrupted by solitary trees on the roadside. The trees became little clusters and then loose congregations and then lined the road like a canopy.

A fox darted across the road and I hit the brakes. The fox looked at me disdainfully as the car ground to halt against the gravel several feet in front of it. As the car skidded to a halt I flailed to my right to grab the flowers. They were loosely wrapped in green wrapping paper and a couple tulips flipped out onto the floor mat. I gathered them up and tried to arrange them back to their original configuration. In spite of my best efforts they looked uneven like when you try to roll toilet paper back onto the roll. I wedged the flowers more securely into the crevice of the seat cushions. In my mind I heard my mother's disapproval that they hadn't been secured well enough in the first place.

She had insisted on tulips. She said they always brought tulips. When I'd gone to the flower shop there was a large grinning woman who smelled of talcum powder behind the counter.

She asked me what I was looking for. I told her "Tulips." She asked what color. I said I didn't know. She smiled at me like you smile at old people who don't know how to use an ATM machine.

"Who are they for?"

"My aunt."

"What does she like?"

"I don't know. She's young."

"Like your age?"

"She was about four I think."

She gave me a puzzled look, but kept her plaster-made smile on all the time. She just nodded like she accepted I was trying to be difficult and picked out some purple and white tulips.

"Do you like these?"

"Yeah, they'll be fine."

I hadn't been to the farmhouse in years. I hoped the pier was still around. I thought I might do a little fishing afterwards if I could. Besides, even futility at fishing would be better than turning around as soon as I finished up at the farm and getting back home at two in the morning. I'd taken an extra day off to do this. I figured I might as well spend a little time relaxing.

I turned off the gravel onto a dirt road. I had a piece of stationary with a crude map and notes that mom had given me to help me find the farmhouse. I couldn't tell what the drawings were supposed to be so I had to try and remember the stories. The rough looking square was the old Baptist Church that had doubled as a one-room schoolhouse that they'd all attended. The line running alongside it was the road I was on. The group of little circles was a rock pile where Seth said he saw a rattlesnake once. On and on, each sketch was a narrative landmark.

I made the last turn and the road turned into two worn dirt grooves in the grass. I came over a small rise and the lake unfolded like a grade school love note. To the right the old barn leaned heavily on its last supports wearily as if it were going to complain that the weather was wreaking havoc with its arthritis. The door was ajar and from what I could see it still was sound enough to sleep in should the situation call for it.

The farmhouse itself burned down three or four years ago. Some high school kids accidentally managed to set it ablaze, destroying the house and giving away the location of their secret bonfire spot to every law enforcement agency and fire department in the county all in one fell swoop. What had been left was bulldozed and the foundation was filled in. You could still see the concrete around the edges of the old foundation like a chalk outline around a body on a TV show. I walked it like a tightrope as grasshoppers clicked and popped around my legs.

I tiptoed gingerly along the concrete edges to the kitchen, back past the pantry to the side door where I finally met up with the remnant of the dirt path that ran down to the lakeside. The sun was hanging just low enough to let other violets and blues begin to creep into the opposite horizon. The breeze coming off the lake was cool but the sun was still hot enough to make my cheeks and forehead feel taut and dry. I navigated the dirt path to the makeshift pier. It was barely standing: planks were missing, one corner had collapsed and it was overrun by reeds. I stood at the edge of the water, the small, subtle gusts of wind were causing little ripples to hiccup and bumble around the cattails and along the shore.

I would have felt more disappointed about the state of the pier but the drive had sobered me up enough to realize that I really didn't want to fish. I'd half-intentionally passed the gas station at the last town instead of buying bait. Funny how some ideas seem so good at the outset and die slow deaths at the hands of a car drive.

I briefly debated about just driving back right away, but my phone had no reception and the technological hum that I'd been neck-deep in for as long as I could remember was gone. It really would've been a shame not to take advantage of the quiet. In spite of my more ambitious plans, deep down this was how I had wanted to spend the evening. I had a cooler with some water, a six-pack of beer, some summer sausage, some cheese, a pack a buns, sunflower seeds and a Snickers bar ready to go. In contrast, I wasn't even sure if I'd remembered the tackle box or not. I'm pretty sure I had but I suppose my disinterest betrayed me.

I wanted to find a smooth stone to try and skip it across the surface of the lake. I remember being ten years old at summer camp and spending hours at the lakeside trying to figure out how to do it. I got it eventually, but never really did it well.

Seth used to be able to get at least eight skips from a rock, no joke. He used to say "You just have to feel it when you throw it." I still don't know what that was supposed to mean.

I poked and prodded with my shoe but only managed to send a couple small frogs fleeing further into the long grass. I remembered being out here as a boy chasing dragonflies. There had been a house here then. Callie had been here too.

Part of me still thinks it's a little creepy. I find urns unsettling, but I'm enough of a modern man to be able to pretend it's a vase. I think of them like canopy beds—they're something some people really like, but that I'm just not meant to understand.

But it I wasn't looking at an urn. In back of the farmyard next to a half-dead chokecherry tree was a little limestone marker.

Callie Marie Weiss
Oct 9, 1948-May 7, 1953

I didn't know my Uncle Seth that well. Mom always talked about him as if he were dead. When she spoke about him it always was about her childhood. She would only talk about Seth as her big brother. When she spoke of him it was only stories from when she was little through when she was in high school when Seth enlisted in the army. She didn't talk about him after he came back. I really only remember seeing him a few times growing up.

He showed up for Christmas one year at my grandparents' when I was in grade school. I remember he was really talkative and laughed louder than anyone. I didn't know what being drunk was. My mother still recalls that Christmas with horror, but Seth was nice to me. He took me out in the yard and pulled me around on a sled behind him and made noises like a horse. After gifts were opened and the adults had shooed us kids away so they could talk in the living room Uncle Seth came down to the basement and played Sorry with us.

That was the night he told me about Callie.

"She was just a little thing. Your grandpa used to say she was no bigger than the nub of his thumb; he called her his little Thumbnub. Your mom ever tell you about her?"

I shook my head "no."

"You knew you had an aunt Callie, right?"

I must have just stared blankly at him for a moment. He looked a little disappointed.

"Well it used to be me, your mom, your aunt Dorsey and your aunt Callie. She was just a little thing, even for her age she was so small but she was fearless. I remember this one time—she couldn't have been more than three—she was chasing a porcupine around the yard. We were all hiding in the barn and yelling at her to come to us. She just laughed at us and chased it some more.

"I went to find dad—your grampa. He was out in the field and I told him Callie was chasing a porcupine. Your grampa, you shoulda seen his face. He had me in the pickup with him in an instant and I never even knew his old truck could move that fast. We came flying into the yard and I don't know who was more scared: me in the truck or that poor porcupine. The porcupine bolted off like it was on fire. My hand hurt from grabbing the arm rest in the truck so hard.

"Dad was out of the truck and scooped up Callie. She had been heading right into the brush after that porcupine. Dad turned and started yelling at me, Dorsey and your mom for not watching Callie better. He seemed mad, but the one who was really mad was Callie. I don't think I've ever seen someone so angry in my life. She was so mad that I'd told dad and that he'd chased away her new friend. She didn't talk to me for two days after that. But that was just Callie.

"She was the one. We thought she'd do something. She was just a force of nature, even at that age. Everyone loved Callie. Just the way she smiled. You knew she was just in that moment and her eyes sparkled. They burned with joy…"

I remember he started coughing in that way people do when they're trying not to throw up.

"Hey, you guys finish up without me. Can't beat you guys at Sorry, you're too good for me. I should go tell your grandma goodbye."

He went upstairs. About an hour later mom came down and asked where he had gone. I told her he had gone to tell grandma goodbye.

But he hadn't. He had just left.

Mom was very specific in her instructions. Specific on the tulips (although apparently not on the color), specific where the marker was and specific on what she wanted me to say.

"You go there and tell her I miss her. You tell her we're all okay—don't tell her anything about your uncle Seth. And you ask Jesus to watch over her."

I imagined if Seth actually made it on his year and Callie really was paying attention she'd know Seth wasn't okay. And the whole Jesus thing—we hadn't stepped inside a church since I was 14. Part of me was tempted to ask Mom if she wanted me to have Santa Claus put a good word in for her while she was at it.

I laid the tulips against the marker. I pulled a couple stray weeds out of the way. Attention to the particulars wasn't really my thing, but it felt right at the time. I traced the outline of the letters with my finger. The rock was a little gritty, not at all smooth like gravestones anymore. It had a more organic, warm feel to it.

I'd grabbed the cooler when I'd picked up the flowers. I popped open a beer and used my pocket knife to hack off a wedge of summer sausage. The treetops behind the grave tangled together into a silhouette of pavement cracks overhead from the backlight of the setting sun.

I'd only seen one picture of Callie. Mom kept it by her bed. It was all of them actually—Mom, Aunt Dorsey, Seth and Callie. It was black and white with a bend in one corner that fissured Dorsey's left side. Mom and Seth had a dog between them that seemed to be looking at something off to the left as Mom had her arm around its neck and Seth held it in place. Callie was out of focus; she had apparently moved so her golden hair was a fuzzy halo around her head. Her limbs looked like they had been frozen in the middle of a clap, as if being stuck in a photo for fifty years was too tiresome to spend the two seconds of stillness required. Seth had been right about her eyes, though. Piercing light blue, they were focused on something near the camera because they were dead-set, hungry and curious.

It wasn't until I was in high school that Mom talked about the grave. I caught her talking in whispers over the phone with Aunt Dorsey. When I asked her about it, she played it off as if it were no big secret—even going so far as to feign surprise that I didn't already know about it. I'd never really wanted to go. It seemed like something between her, Dorsey and Seth and if experience was any indication, family things that involved Seth were best avoided at all costs.

The frogs and crickets joined in chorus as the sky turned pink and red with the waning of the daylight. A few rogue planets and stars began to appear on the far horizon. The moon had been around since that afternoon, like the guy who shows up too early for a party, standing in a corner, nursing a warm beer until everyone else gets there so he can cut loose.

I was down three beers by the time the moon began dancing with the other arrivals. I arranged the flowers again, a little more upright this time. I stood in front of the little grave marker and cleared my throat, feeling a little nervous.

"Mom wanted me to tell you that everyone misses you. We're all doing okay. Jesus will be watching over you."

I stood there for a moment, reflecting on the aunt I had never known. I wondered how things would have been different if she'd lived. I wondered if she would have been everything Seth believed she would be. No way of knowing, I suppose. But she had been enough to keep Mom, Dorsey and even Seth coming to check on her year after year. That was miracle enough, I thought.

I spread out my bedroll and laid out facing the sky. I could find Cassiopeia and Orion. Then I followed the edge of the Big Dipper to the North Star and then let my eyes wander across other forms that I'd never learned. There was a totality to all of it—the expanse of the sky, the breeze across my face and the cool grass tickling at the back of my neck. I could see why they chose to bury Callie here. Each night the quiet isolation would usher in something so magnificent and you could almost hear the air sigh gently. At least that's how it looked from where I was lying.

Across the water I could hear a chorus of frogs and crickets chirping their separate songs. The leaves clapped softly as the wind danced through the branches and the air smelled of damp earth and tree bark.

And the stars sparkled and burned with joy.

Also by the author:

All Things Right and Beautiful

All the Stupid Little Children